Pearl's Pirates

OTHER YEARLING BOOKS YOU WILL ENJOY:

YEARLING BOOKS/YOUNG YEARLINGS/YEARLING CLASSICS are designed especially to entertain and enlighten young people. Patricia Reilly Giff, consultant to this series, received the bachelor's degree from Marymount College. She holds the master's degree in history from St. John's University, and a Professional Diploma in Reading from Hofstra University. She was a teacher and reading consultant for many years, and is the author of numerous books for young readers.

For a complete listing of all Yearling titles, write to
Dell Readers Service, P.O. Box 1045,
South Holland, IL 60473.

Pearl's Pirates

written and illustrated by
FRANK ASCH

A Yearling Book

Published by
Dell Publishing
a division of
Bantam Doubleday Dell Publishing Group, Inc.
666 Fifth Avenue
New York, New York 10103

ISBN: 0-440-40245-X

Reprinted by arrangement with Delacorte Press

Printed in the United States of America

December 1989

10 9 8 7 6 5 4 3 2 1

CWO

to Leigh Dean

(1)

JAY WAS RIDING HIS BIKE AND WE WERE IN HIS JACKET pocket nibbling on a peanut when all of a sudden— WHAM—everything went blank. When I awoke I was lying on the side of the road and Wilbur was standing over me.

"Pearl, are you okay? Can you hear me?"

"Yeah, I'm all right," I said, rubbing the bump on my head. "What happened? Where's Jay?"

"Oh, Pearl, it was horrible! There was blood on his head and his arm dangled down like it was broken . . . and . . ."

"But what happened?" I cried. "Where is he?"

"Hit and run, that's what it was," moaned Wilbur. "I saw the whole thing. The driver of the car didn't even stop."

"And Jay?"

"A lady driving a blue truck stopped. A few minutes later an ambulance came. It all happened so fast! Next

thing I knew they were taking Jay to the hospital. I wanted to go with him, but I had to stay with you. Oh, Pearl, I thought you might be dead!"

I couldn't believe what I was hearing. Our Jay was hurt . . . hurt bad. The tears welled up inside of me, but I fought to keep them down. Standing up tall on my hind paws, I took a good look around. Everywhere I turned there was nothing but highway, grass, and trees, none of which looked familiar. "There's no way we could get to the hospital. I don't even know how to get home from here."

"It will be getting dark soon," said Wilbur. "I think we ought to find some shelter."

On the other side of the road was a fallen tree with roots that stuck out of the ground. A tractor-trailer truck rumbled past, then a car.

"After this one," I said, checking in both directions. When we got to the other side of the road, we dashed into the roots of the old tree.

"I guess we'll have to wait till Jay comes back to look for us. There's probably lots to eat in the fields around here," said Wilbur, carefully sniffing the air. "I smell some corn, and there's a stream that way . . . and . . . wait a minute"—Wilbur lifted his nose to get a better scent—"I smell something else too . . . smells like . . . rats! And they're coming this way!"

Two rats were traveling in the ditch not far from where we were hidden. As they passed by one of them found something good to eat and they started fighting over it. Growling like mad dogs, they thrashed about in the weeds until one of them managed to snatch the prize.

"Aw come on, Bones, gimme some of that," snarled one rat. "I ain't had a peanut in months."

"Back off, Scrags!" snapped the rat called Bones, and we listened while he devoured the nut in one bite. "There'll be plenty more grub at the mouse party tonight."

"That must be *our* peanut, the one Jay gave us," I whispered to Wilbur.

"Shhh," he replied, "they'll hear us."

"Yeah, tell me *again* about the mouse party," pleaded Scrags.

"We meet in the rusty old truck by the big warehouse," said Bones, "and we stay hid until the town clock strikes nine."

"How come we gotta wait?"

" 'Cause Boss Rat wants to make sure all the mice are in the crate before we attack. Now shut yer yap and listen, 'cause I ain't gonna tell ya again. Ahem, where was I? Oh yeah . . . then we move in, bust 'em up, and have a feast!"

"I like that part," said Scrags. "Now tell me the other part."

"Ah, Scrags, I told you a million times already!"

"One more time, please, Bones?"

"Okay, one more time, but that's it," snapped Bones. "And Boss Rat says if we do good tonight, *maybe* we can join the pack."

"Well chop my tail with a meat cleaver! If that ain't

every rat's dream . . . to be in the pack with Boss Rat! Tell me that part *one* more time, please, Bones."

"No way. If I spend all night telling ya about it, we'll never get there!" declared Bones. And we heard the two rats scamper away.

For a full minute or so we didn't move or speak for fear that the rats might return. Then Wilbur said, "I'd hate to be in that warehouse at nine o'clock. Those mice are in for a heap of trouble."

"Maybe we ought to try and warn them, Wilbur. What do you think?"

"Wouldn't be hard to track the rats to the warehouse," said Wilbur. "But could we get in, warn the mice at the party, and get out before the rats attacked? That's the question."

"I know we've got our own problems right now, Wilbur," I said, "but don't you think we ought to try?"

Wilbur wrinkled up his nose, squeezed his eyes shut, and moaned, "I can't stand it. One nightmare's not over yet and another one begins!"

After we climbed out of the roots we took a few moments to look around so we would be sure to remember this spot when we returned. Then we set out after the rats. The rats' scent was fresh and easy to track, especially for Wilbur, who has a fantastic sense of smell. Sometimes I think he could smell a piece of cheddar cheese from a mile away and tell you if it was mild or sharp.

A few hundred yards from the old tree the rats left the ditch and cut across the road onto some old railroad tracks. The tracks were covered with weeds, wild-flowers, and bits of junk. When we came upon an old hubcap filled with rainwater, we stopped for a drink. Having quenched my thirst, I noticed my reflection in the water. I looked so scared, it frightened me. Then I realized it wasn't my reflection I was looking at but Wilbur's!

Leaving the railroad tracks, the rats meandered through a junkyard and cut across an open lot. On the far end of the lot was a large brick building. It had few windows and a flat roof.

"That must be the warehouse," I said.

"Look over there. The rusty old truck," said Wilbur. "Can you smell them? There must be two dozen rats in there!"

The warehouse had several metal doors, the kind that roll down in sections. One of the doors was broken. Instead of closing firmly to the ground like the others, it left a space at the bottom large enough to crawl under. We were about to go in when Wilbur stopped dead in his tracks.

"No! It's too dangerous. Come on, let's get out of here!"

"But, Wilbur, those mice need our help!"

"I know! I know!" cried Wilbur. "But I can't go in there. I'm too scared!"

A few feet from the door I noticed a thin metal pipe. I walked over to it. "Crawl in here, Wilbur. It's small enough so no rat will be able to get at you. If any mice come along, warn them. I'll go inside and tell the others."

CRRRRSLANK! We heard a loud noise. Spinning around, I saw a loose section of drainpipe swinging in the breeze and banging against the building. When I turned back, Wilbur had disappeared into the pipe.

"You'll be safe here. I'll be right back," I called to him, and ducked under the door into the warehouse.

I didn't like leaving Wilbur behind, but the rats said they would attack at nine, and I was afraid time was running out.

The warehouse was so large, once I was inside, it almost felt like I was outside again. Everywhere I looked huge wooden crates stacked like building blocks loomed overhead. Above them were skylights with many panes of frosted glass. Following the strong scent of mouse, I made my way toward the front of the building. There I came upon an old man sleeping in an armchair. He was wearing a dark green watchman's uniform. Curled up next to his feet was a large German shepherd. They were both asleep, but I wasn't taking any chances. Keeping one eye on the dog, I made a wide circle around them.

As I went down one row of crates, then another, the smell of mouse grew stronger and stronger. I could almost make out the scent of individual mice but something was jamming the signal—something like perfume. Finally I turned a corner and spotted a very unusual crate.

At first glance it looked like any of the others. Made

of rough-cut pine boards, it had metal brackets on all of its corners. Sturdy wire bands ran from top to bottom, and the word FRAGILE was stenciled on every side. But on its bottommost board, a few inches from the floor, was a small knothole. Through the knothole I saw a flickering yellow light and heard music mixed with the voices of many mice.

Drawing closer, I entered.

"Welcome to the party!" two dancing mice greeted me at the knothole. "There's plenty of food. Just help yourself!"

I tried to speak with them, but before I could open my mouth they danced off.

The crate contained a large antique table. It was a fancy table with legs that looked like lion's paws balanced on a tennis ball. At the far end of the crate were several bottles of perfume. No doubt that's what was confusing my nose. Near each of the four legs of the table were piles and piles of food. There was chocolate, cheese, crackers, nuts, bits of bacon, crusts of bread, candied fruit, roots and seeds, and cereals, and so much more I couldn't possibly mention it all. On the floor of the crate beneath the table was a lit candle. It was small but shed a great deal of light. Next to the candle was a unique musical combo, a bullfrog-cricket band. A bright green bullfrog sat in the center of the group. While the frog, wearing a serious expression on his face, croaked out a steady even beat, the crickets played the most delightful melodies. Around the bullfrog-cricket band danced dozens of mice. As they hopped and swayed, their shadows flickered against the wall of the crate.

Pushing past the dancers, I moved toward the band looking for someone to tell about the rats. I hadn't gone far when someone called my name.

"Pearl!"

The voice sounded so familiar. I turned and was utterly dumbfounded. Standing before me was my little brother, Tony!

(2)

I WAS SO EXCITED, HAD I BEEN A POT OF WATER I would have boiled away to nothing. "Tony! What are you doing here?" I cried, and gave him a great big mouse hug.

Tony is my youngest brother. Last fall, after I helped him escape from Adams's Pet Store, I left him living with two kindly old field mice, Oliver and Josephine.

"I don't live in the country anymore. I'm a town mouse now," replied Tony boldly.

"But, Tony, I thought you loved living in the field. What happened? Did you have trouble finding enough food to get you through the winter? Was it too cold?"

"No, I had plenty of food and I was very warm and cozy in my burrow," sighed Tony.

"Then what was it? Did you have a fight with Oliver and Josephine?"

Tony shrugged his shoulders and looked down at his paws.

"No, we got along fine, in fact I miss them both. But I can't go back there."

I could tell Tony was reluctant to talk about his reason for leaving the field. But I felt I had to know. "Why, Tony?" I pressed him.

"It was right after all the snow melted." Tony heaved a big sigh. "I was out looking for something green to munch on. I was about to jump down onto a big black rock when I realized it wasn't a rock at all—it was a big black garter snake. I ran back to my burrow and stayed there all day. I knew it was nothing to worry about, just another predator to keep an eye on, but it gave me such terrible nightmares! I couldn't stop dreaming about what happened in Adams's Pet Store. So I had to leave. You understand, don't you, Pearl?"

"Yes, I understand," I replied, and a cold shiver ran down my spine as I remembered Mr. Adams's attempt to feed Tony to his new python.

"Actually, I've only been in town for a few days. I'm staying with Albert and Vera until I get settled," said Tony. Albert is my older brother, and Vera is the streetwise gray mouse that he befriended after the big escape from Adams's Pet Store.

"Are they here too?" I asked.

"Yes, they're dancing," replied Tony, pointing into the crowd.

"Where? I don't see them." I peered into the swirling mass of tails, ears, and whiskers trembling with anticipation. For a moment I thought Tony was teasing me, then Albert's white fur came into view and I rushed over to greet them. Right in the middle of the dance floor, with everyone bumping into us, we all rubbed whiskers and hugged one another.

Then Wilbur's sister, Lucy, appeared. When she lived with us in the pet store, she spent most of her time peering through the bars of our cage watching Mr. Adams's TV. Perfume and fashion commercials were her favorite things to watch. Now her toenails were painted bright red and she reeked of perfume. Standing by her side was her friend, the great Shakespearean mouse-actor, Frederic French.

"We are honored indeed!" intoned Frederic with a gracious bow.

"How nice of you to come all this way to attend our going-away party," exclaimed Lucy.

"Actually, I didn't know it was your party," I said.

"Oh," said Lucy, as if I had insulted her.

"The address on the crate says Paris, France," explained Frederic. "We expect to be leaving any day now. We decided it was high time for a little vacation, a chance to relax and recharge the batteries of creativity. And I want Lucy to see Europe the way I remember it, that is before it's completely commercialized. Shakespeare had quite a few things to say about travel. Permit me to recite you a few lines—"

"Excuse me, Frederic"—I interrupted him as politely as I could—"but I think there's something you all ought to know," and I proceeded to tell everyone about the rats.

"Rats! We didn't invite any rats!" declared Lucy. "How dare they intrude! This is a private party!"

"No, of course you didn't invite them," said Vera. "But that won't stop them from coming in here, eating our food, and wrecking everything in sight!"

"It's too bad," grumbled Albert. "The rats in this town are really a menace! I'd like to see them get a taste of their own medicine for a change."

"Yeah, let's fight 'em tooth and tail!" declared Tony.

"That's not exactly what I had in mind," replied Albert. "I was thinking about that watchdog. If only we could get him to chase the rats away." Albert paused to think for a moment. "Yes! It would work! All we have to do is station ourselves by the dog. When the town clock strikes nine, the rats will attack, but they won't be able to get into the crate until they enlarge the hole. Not even the tiniest rat could fit through there. That will give us plenty of time to wake up the dog and get him to chase us to the crate."

"Let the dog take care of the rats! Great idea!" exclaimed Vera.

"Splendid!" said Frederic. "But as host and hostess, Lucy and I should remain with our guests."

"Don't worry about a thing," said Albert. "Vera and I will wake up the dog and your party can go on as planned."

"Actually, it's better to do this kind of thing with three or four mice," said Vera. "That way, if the dog gets too close, we can always scatter."

"Can I come?" asked Tony.

"Most certainly not," snapped Albert. "This may be a dangerous operation."

"But it's not fair," grumbled Tony. "You guys always get to have all the fun."

"I promise we won't have any fun," said Albert in his best big-brother voice.

"Pearl, tell him I can come," begged Tony.

But I had to agree with Albert. Tony is not only a lot younger than we are, he also has a tendency to take foolish risks merely to prove his bravery.

"I think it would be better if you kept an eye on things here," I said.

"Do you want to come with us, Pearl?" asked Vera. "We'll need at least three to do this right."

"Well . . ." I hesitated, thinking about Wilbur still waiting outside for me in the pipe.

"Not afraid, are you?" asked Albert.

"No, I'm not afraid," I replied firmly.

"Then come on," said Vera, leading the way. "If I'm not mistaken, I heard the town clock strike eight some time ago."

Vera knew a shortcut. After leaving the crate instead of going down the aisles, she led us on a zigzag route, squeezing between the crates. In practically no time at all we stepped out into the open and found ourselves standing before the watchman and his dog.

"This reminds me of the old days, when I was growing up downtown," said Vera. "We used to do this sort of thing just for fun."

BONG, BONG, BONG, the town clock began to strike.

"Wait here, I'll wake him up," said Albert.

"No, let me do it," argued Vera. "You don't know the first thing about waking up a dog." . . . BONG, BONG, BONG . . .

"Sure I do!" replied Albert. "Holler in his ear."

"No, no, you've got to pull his whiskers!" exclaimed Vera.

While Vera and Albert bickered about which one of them was going to wake up the dog, I stood there shivering with fright. We were already so close to the dog, I could feel his warm breath. Each time he exhaled it covered us like a balmy breeze. Standing next to that mountain of fur, I remembered the time Jay's friend Billy Chase took us out of our cage and held us up close so his puppy could sniff us. That was scary, but nothing compared to this. . . . BONG, BONG, BONG.

Finally Albert and Vera resolved their argument and agreed to wake up the dog together.

"Watch us, and be ready to run," said Albert, and they both edged forward until they reached the dog's muzzle. Going around to either side, they stood up on their hind legs. Pausing for a moment, they looked over at me to make sure I was ready, then they grabbed hold of the dog's whiskers and yanked with all their might.

Instantly the dog awoke and jerked back his head. Dazed, he bared his teeth.

"Grrrrrr!" he growled, and sprang to his feet. But Vera and Albert were already on the run.

"Rrrwoof, Rrrwoof, Rrrwoof!"

I felt the dog's bark zing through my body like an electric shock.

"Run!" cried Albert.

Everything was going according to Albert's plan. The dog was up, but we had a good head start.

Then—CRASH!—we heard a terrible racket.

"Aaahhh!" the old man screamed.

"Hold it, everybody!" cried Vera.

I stopped and spun around.

Apparently there was one major flaw in Albert's plan. The dog was chained to the watchman's chair! When he lit out after us, he yanked the chair right out from under his startled master and dumped him on the floor.

Barking wildly, the dog dragged the chair along the floor until it wedged between two crates. The watchman, unhurt, jumped up and turned on his powerful flashlight.

"Down, boy!" he commanded, beaming the flashlight into our eyes. "It's only mice."

Cussing to himself, the watchman picked up his chair and tied the dog's chain to a metal post. Eager to chase us, the dog continued to bark until the watchman sat down and petted him.

"Easy, boy. Go back to sleep! It's only mice," he said again and again, until finally the dog settled down. Then the watchman turned off his flashlight.

"Oh rats!" cried Albert. "We should have noticed the chain!"

"To the crate!" cried Vera, running at full speed. "Maybe it's not too late!"

Toenails tapping on the cement floor like tiny little drumrolls, we ran as fast as we could, but not fast enough. Skidding around the corner, we came to a sudden stop. The rats had already attacked!

(3)

IT WAS SENSELESS TO EVEN THINK ABOUT FIGHTING THE rats. So we hid ourselves behind a metal post to watch and wait. One rat was twice as big and ten times as ugly as any of the others.

"That's Boss Rat," said Vera. "He's a real cat-killer."

As Albert had predicted, the rats couldn't fit through the knothole, but two rats were already at work making it larger.

"I've seen worms chew faster. Speed it up!" snarled Boss Rat.

"Yes, Boss! Right away, Boss!" replied one of the rats gnawing at the knothole.

"We're working on it, Boss!" said the other rat. As soon as they spoke I recognized the two rats as Bones and Scrags, the very rats Wilbur and I overheard when we were hiding in the roots of the old tree.

"Stand back!" snapped Boss Rat as he paced back and forth impatiently. "I need room to think!"

Except for Bones and Scrags, the other rats retreated, forming a wide semicircle around the knothole.

Stepping up to the opening, Boss Rat cleared his throat.

"Listen, you moles, this is Boss Rat! You know who I am? I'm the biggest, meanest rat there ever was or will be. I'm so tough, my mother don't even like me. Nobody or nothin' likes me 'cause I'm rotten-mean. Why I can't even drink milk, 'cause every time I look at it, it curdles and turns to cheese."

The other rats were so pleased and tickled by what Boss Rat said, they poked one another in the ribs and snickered out loud.

"Shut up," said Boss Rat, and instantly silenced the pack. "Now where was I? Oh, yeah, I'm mean, but right now I'm more hungry than mean, and it's taking too long to make this knothole big enough for a rat like me. So send out some food right now! Ya hear me? Right now—and who knows, maybe I'll go easy on ya!"

"No! Go away! Go away or you'll be sorry," said a voice from inside the crate.

"Why, that's Tony's voice!" exclaimed Vera.

Boss Rat was outraged.

"Nobody, but nobody, talks to Boss Rat that way! Ya hear me? Nobody!" he sputtered indignantly.

"I said, leave us alone. Go away!" cried Tony.

"You die, you all die, ya hear me. . . . You Die!" ranted Boss Rat. "I'll squeeze your guts, I'll crush your skull, I'll pick my teeth with your whiskers! . . ." He

went on and on, talking so fast and angrily I couldn't understand half of what he said.

When he was finished, Tony called out, "Leave us alone. I'm warning you."

This time Boss Rat merely stepped back into his pack and commanded Bones and Scrags, "Chew!"

"Tony's got spunk. I'll always remember him that way," said Albert dryly.

It was only a matter of time before the knothole was large enough for the rats to slip through. Then the massacre would begin.

Suddenly Bones and Scrags jumped back from the knothole.

"What's going on here?" barked Boss Rat, sniffing and curling his upper lip. "What's that smell?"

"It's Lucy's perfume," whispered Vera. "Tony must have squirted some through the knothole."

"Don't you smell sweet! OOOoooeeeEEE!" The other rats started teasing Bones and Scrags.

"Keep chewing!" commanded Boss Rat.

"Please, Boss, don't make us!"

"What's the matter? Don't you want to smell nice for the party?" sassed one of the rats from the pack.

"Chew!" commanded Boss Rat.

Once again Tony sprayed some perfume out the knothole. Bones and Scrags stepped farther back.

"You wanna join this pack, don't ya?" threatened Boss Rat.

"Oh yes, Boss, you know we do!" replied Bones.

"Then you gotta follow orders. And my orders are to chew! Ya hear me? Chew!"

"Please, Boss, we'll do anything . . . chase cats . . . kill chickens . . . anything you say, but not that!" pleaded Bones.

"Don't we smell bad enough already?" added Scrags.

"Do it!" Boss Rat shook with rage.

"Come on," said Bones, "we'd better get out of here," and the two rats ran into the shadows of the warehouse.

"Leave now and you'll never join the pack!" Boss Rat called after them, but they did not reply and they did not turn back.

"Where you going, sissy-sweet?" the other rats called into the darkness. "Come back, flower, we want another sniff!"

Boss Rat was so furious, he snapped his teeth and scratched the cement floor with his claws. But no one obeyed his command to take up where Bones and Scrags had left off. None of the other rats would even go near the knothole. For a moment it seemed like Boss Rat would enlarge the hole himself. He took a few steps forward but then stopped. Apparently the fear of smelling pretty was too much for even Boss Rat!

"Mice, lice, what's the difference, let's go to the dump to get some decent grub!" he declared.

The other rats grumbled, "What, no feast?"

But when Boss Rat turned and walked away, they all followed. In a few minutes the entire warehouse was free of rats and we were able to go back to the crate.

(4)

As soon as we entered the crate Lucy and Frederic greeted us with big smiles.

"We were truly concerned for your safety," said Frederic.

"What happened to the watchdog?" Lucy wanted to know. "If Tony hadn't thought of using my perfume bottle, this party would have been a dreadful failure!"

Tony beamed with pride. "I guess it's a good thing I didn't go with you guys after all, isn't it?" he boasted.

Albert nodded silently but said nothing.

"Well, come on, everybody," exclaimed Frederic, "the night is still young and the festivities have hardly begun!"

The party had become more than just a farewell party for Lucy and Frederic, it was a celebration of victory over the rats! The bullfrog band played louder than ever and a cheer rose up for Tony:

"Hip, Hip, Hooray!
He did it with perfume spray!

Three cheers for the mouse of the day!
Hip, Hip, Hooray!
Hip, Hip, Hooray!
Hip, Hip, Hooray!"

They cheered again and again, until finally they hoisted Tony up onto their shoulders and danced him around the candle.

"Something to eat?" asked Vera, coming over with a large chunk of Jarlsberg cheese. "Taste this! Albert and I brought it from the deli."

"Maybe later, Vera," I whispered. "I left my friend Wilbur hiding in a pipe outside and I want to get him before I do anything else."

"Why are you whispering?" asked Vera, who had never met Wilbur.

"Because my friend was too afraid to come in when the rats were around, and I don't think he'd want the others to know."

"Oh." Vera nodded understandingly.

"Holy Swiss cheese, look who's here! It's Wilbur!" cried Tony.

Wearing a sheepish grin on his face, Wilbur pushed through the crowd and came toward us.

"Well, if it isn't my long lost brother!" cried Lucy.

"Hi, Sis," said Wilbur, and they rubbed whiskers and hugged.

"You okay?" I asked.

"Yeah, I'm all right," answered Wilbur pensively.

"What happened? I saw the rats go in, then after a while I saw them leave in a huff."

"Let me tell him!" cried Tony.

While Tony told the tale of his brave encounter with Boss Rat, Vera passed around the cheese.

"I'll bet your little boy doesn't give you anything *that* good," said Albert.

"He sure does! Every night after dinner he comes upstairs and gives us a little something that he saves from his plate," I said.

Of course everyone wanted to know how it happened that Wilbur and I had come to be at the party.

When I finished telling our story, carefully leaving out the part about Wilbur hiding in the pipe, Vera said, "It must have been a terrible experience for you."

"What are you going to do now?" asked Tony.

"What a silly question," snapped Albert. "Of course, they're going to come live with us in the deli."

"Actually we were planning on going back to Jay," said Wilbur.

"You mean you really *like* being *pet mice!*" exclaimed Albert.

The way he said "pet mice" made my fur crawl.

"And what's so wrong with being a pet mouse?" I asked.

"Oh nothing . . . nothing at all . . . if you like living in cages, that is," snickered Albert. "Does he still call you George?" (Albert was referring to the fact that when Jay bought me, Mr. Adams told him I was a boy mouse, so Jay named me George.)

"As a matter of fact, he does," I replied coolly.

Albert grinned and turned to Wilbur. "And what does he call you?"

"None of your business," said Wilbur.

"Aw, come on, you can tell me," coaxed Albert.

"Promise you won't laugh?" insisted Wilbur.

"Cross my heart and hope to die in a mousetrap," pledged Albert.

"Well . . . okay," said Wilbur, swallowing nervously, "he calls me . . . Sally."

"Ah, ha-ha-ha." Albert actually fell over, he laughed so hard.

Wilbur scrunched his face up like a piece of crumpled paper and shot Albert the dirtiest look I ever saw.

I hadn't seen Albert for months, and he had already succeeded in making me very angry.

"Do you still go to the library to read?" I asked Vera, hastily changing the subject.

"Oh yes!" replied Vera. "And I don't just read book titles anymore, but whole books from cover to cover. Albert and I read together sometimes, but my favorite subject is history, and Albert doesn't like it very much."

"I find it depressing," said Albert in a serious tone of voice. "History . . . what is it? . . . one war after another, people fighting people . . . like rats! Who needs it? Too bad there's no such subject as mousetory."

"There's mystery," I said.

"Not the same thing," replied Albert. "Say, did you know I've written a book?" (I always wondered what would come of Albert's self-taught ability to write with his tail.)

"That's terrific, Albert. What's your book about?" I asked.

"It's about people," said Albert. "I watch them all day long in the deli and write up my observations at night. I believe it's the first truly scientific study of people that's ever been written."

"Oh, come on," challenged Wilbur, "surely there have been other scientific books written about people."

"Yes, but all of them were written by *other* people and therefore not scientifically objective!" declared Albert.

"But I've read your book," argued Vera, "and I don't think it's very objective. How could it be with a title like *People, Vermin of the Earth?*"

"I write what I see," said Albert. "It's not my fault people are so rotten. But it's not enough to merely describe the problem. Something has to be done about it! That's what my new book is going to be about. Only yesterday I started chapter one. I call it my *Mouseifesto.* It's a call to mice around the world to put aside their differences and unite to overthrow the tyrannical rule of mankind."

"Are you trying to suggest that mice should take over the world?" I asked.

"Precisely!" exclaimed Albert. "Why, did you know that two grown mice, if left alone for one year, can have a million descendants! Just think of what an army we mice could raise if only we could get organized. There'd be no stopping us. I can see it now, whole cellars full of mice all over the world marching up the stairs and taking over!"

"I have to confess it sounds pretty farfetched to me," I told Albert.

"Of course we'll have to start *small*," said Albert, "but you'll see, once my *Mouseifesto* is finished, everything will change."

"I wish you could meet Jay sometime," I said. "He's not rotten."

"You guys still talking?" cried Tony, running over to us with a big piece of chocolate in his paws. "Better eat up, the food is going fast."

Tony was right. Now that the party was in full swing, the food piles had dwindled to half their former size. Especially when the bullfrog-cricket band took a break, all the dancers began to eat like crazy.

When the bullfrog, in a lapse of good manners, ate one of the crickets, the other crickets refused to play anymore. But another group, a barbershop quartet, took their place. They called themselves The Micetros. For the most part they sang old favorites, but they also mixed in a few original tunes. One was quite memorable. It went something like this:

My love she is so pretty,
The cutest mouse in town.
Her whiskers are so long,
Her ears so big and round.
I gave her flowers

One two three,
Candies four five six,
But she would not marry me
Oh my, what a fix!
So while she slept in a cooking pot,
I crept up to her side,
Tied our tails in a sailor's knot
and now she is my bride.
And our children are so pretty,
The cutest mice in to-o-own,
Their whiskers are so long,
Their ears so big and ro-o-ound.

"Oh, Albert," said Vera as we listened to the crooning Micetros, "wouldn't it be nice to go to France with Frederic and Lucy?"

"Maybe after I finish my *Mouseifesto,*" said Albert, "we'll take a long vacation. Yes, that's it. We'll go around the world. I'll bring my *Mouseifesto.* We'll hold meetings and I'll read it out loud."

"Doesn't sound very romantic to me," sighed Vera.

"Don't worry"—Albert gave her a little kiss—"we'll have fun, too, you'll see."

Everyone loved the Micetros, but when all the food was gone, the party began to break up. Wishing Frederic and Lucy well on their trip to France, mouse after mouse exited through the knothole.

We didn't know the way to Jay's house from the scene of the accident, but I was pretty sure I still remembered the way from the deli, so I asked Albert and Vera if we could go home with them.

"Sure," replied Albert. "The only problem is that we promised Frederic and Lucy that we'd sleep over and help them clean up in the morning. It was Vera's idea . . . sort of a going-away gift."

"Splendid! Why don't you all spend the night?" exclaimed Frederic. "Tomorrow we'll have brunch together."

"That sounds good to me," yawned Wilbur. "I'm exhausted."

Tony, curled up around the burned-out candle, was already snoring. Though tired, I was also very restless and did not fall asleep right away. Wilbur couldn't sleep either.

"I'm sorry about what happened this afternoon," said Wilbur. "I guess I just lost my nerve for a while. Without Jay around I feel scared all the time. I keep thinking something is going to jump out and grab me."

"No need to apologize," I said. "I felt the same way the first time I went out on my own."

"I know, but I still feel kind of bad about it. Does anyone else know what happened?" asked Wilbur.

"Only Vera," I replied, "but I told her not to spread it around."

"I hope Albert doesn't find out," yawned Wilbur. "He'd tease me for sure."

Soon Wilbur was asleep, but I was still feeling restless. I kept thinking back on the events of the day. And what a day it had been! First there had been the accident, then the rats . . . but now it seemed like events were taking a turn for the better. At least Wilbur and I would be able to get back to Jay's house. We could get in through the cellar. Jay's mom would put us back in our cage and take care of us. When Jay got back from the hospital, we'd be there to greet him. It was a comforting thought. At last I closed my eyes and fell asleep, thinking how nice it would be to see Jay again.

I had many dreams that night. Some good, some bad, but none of them as bad as what really happened in the morning.

THUD! THUD! THUD! I nearly jumped out of my skin. Someone was banging on the side of the crate. I rubbed my eyes, still full of sleep, and stared at the shiny tips of nails as they thrust through the side of the crate around the knothole.

"The knothole! Oh no!" cried Wilbur. "Someone's boarded up the knothole!"

(5)

"THAT OUGHT TO KEEP THOSE MICE OUT!" SAID A MAN'S voice.

"Looks like the teeth marks of a rat to me," said another man's voice.

"Rats, mice, chipmunks, what's the difference? Let's get this crate loaded," said the first voice. "Lift on the count of three. Ready? One, two, three!"

"What's happening?" cried Tony.

"I think we're being carried somewhere," said Albert.

"Not just somewhere!" exclaimed Frederic. "We're on our way to Paris, France! Isn't it splendid?"

"Oh no," moaned Wilbur. "Are you sure? Couldn't they be shuffling the crates around or something?"

I was hoping against hope that Wilbur was right, but when the men set the crate down, we heard the sound of an engine starting and the crate began to jiggle and shake.

"We must be in a truck. They really are taking us to France!" I cried.

"But France is across the ocean. How are they going to drive us there?" asked Tony.

"Silly mouse," exclaimed Lucy, "they're going to take us to the dock and put us on a ship, and the ship will sail us to France."

"Are there snakes in France?" Tony wanted to know.

"Yes, but I don't think you'll have to worry about them in Paris," said Frederic. "Oh, this *is* splendid! Just think of it! Paris in the springtime . . . strolling down the Champs Élysées . . . visiting the Louvre . . . and the Eiffel Tower . . . the cultural experience of a lifetime!"

"Looks like we're going to take a vacation after all," said Vera to Albert.

"But I've only just started my *Mouseifesto!* My ink, my paper, everything I need is in the deli! I say we chew our way out!" exclaimed Albert, and he walked over to the wall of the crate, picked a spot, and started to gnaw.

I don't think I have to tell you how Wilbur and I felt. Our one burning desire was to get back to Jay. Before Albert had taken two bites we were by his side chewing like we had never chewed before. Each time we bit down we made a little progress. But chewing through wood is never easy. Every time the truck hit a bump our teeth would slip. Soon we had a little pile of wood chips and a not so deep gash in the side of the crate. When Albert and Wilbur got tired, Tony and

Vera took a turn. But neither Frederic nor Lucy lent a tooth.

"Chew wood like a common termite?" said Lucy. "I wouldn't think of such a thing!"

An hour passed, maybe more. Then the truck stopped. We heard doors slamming, and once again the workmen carted us somewhere. As they jostled us along thin slivers of sunlight seeped through the cracks in the crate.

"I smell salt air," said Wilbur. "We must be at the dock."

Then we heard the sound of clanking chains and it felt like we were being lifted up into the air. We heard crowds of people below us and gulls flying near. Suspended in midair, the crate rocked back and forth and began to descend. The slivers of sunlight disappeared. The crate came to rest and the workmen took off the chains.

Through all of this we never stopped chewing. We gnawed until it hurt to talk and it felt like our teeth would fall out. We chomped till our jaws felt like pudding. We didn't give up until we had a hole large enough for a mouse to crawl through. It took a long time, but we did it!

"Well, shall we go out and see where we are?" said Vera, spitting one last wood chip from her mouth. "Who wants to go first?"

"I will," answered Tony, and he dashed out of the hole.

One by one, we followed.

At first I thought we were in another warehouse and breathed a sigh of relief. Everywhere I looked there were nothing but crates stacked up to the ceiling. "It will be difficult getting home from this strange warehouse, but at least we're not on a ship bound for France," I told myself. Only one thing worried me—a low vibrating hum. "Could it be the sound of a ship's engine?" I wondered.

Lucy and Frederic were the last to leave the crate.

"I do thank you all for making such a splendid little exit for us," said Frederic, sniffing the air more like a gentleman taking snuff than a mouse.

"But where are we?" Tony wanted to know.

"I'd say we're in the cargo hold of a big ship, probably an ocean liner," guessed Albert.

"You've got a bingo there!" said a strange voice from up above. Startled, we all looked to its source as a thin brown mouse climbed down from the crate facing our own. It was the oldest mouse I had ever seen. He had a roundish head, long fur, and a laundry basket full of wrinkles under his eyes.

"Who are you?" gasped Albert.

"They used to call me Billy Boy, then it was just Bill, now they call me Old Bill," said the ancient mouse.

Acting as our self-appointed spokesmouse, Frederic introduced us and gave a long-winded account of how we got trapped in the crate.

"Reminds me of the time I fell down a well," said Old Bill. "Woulda drowned if I didn't hold on to a piece of bark. Sailed that scrap of wood for weeks living

on moss and snails, waiting for someone to crank up the bucket."

"Do you live here?" I inquired politely.

"Yes, lass, that I do," replied the old mouse. "Used to have a little boat of my own. Her name was *Gertrude*. You might say she was a toy boat. But she was a real boat for me. Sailed the seven seas seven times each, we did. Up the Hudson and down the Nile . . . ah, those were the days! But I lost her in a storm off the coast of Portugal. Poor dear, I hated to see her go down." Old Bill heaved a deep sigh of remembering. "Got another boat for a while, but it weren't the same. That tub never did steer right, always veered to the starboard whenever the wind kicked up. Got so disgusted I chewed a hole in her bow myself. Boat like that don't deserve to sail the same waters as *Gertrude*. Now I'm retired, living the easy life down here."

"Very interesting," said Albert, though he didn't seem interested at all. "We'd like to get back to shore as soon as possible. Could you tell us how to get off this ship?"

"Sorry, mate," replied Old Bill. "But I reckon we've left the harbor and the tugs have all gone back."

"Then that sound we hear . . . ?" I felt a terrible sinking feeling in the pit of my stomach.

" 'Tis the sound of the ship's engines, lass," said Old Bill.

"Can't we swim ashore?" asked Wilbur.

"Been a sailor for a long time," said Old Bill, "but I never met a mouse that could swim that far."

"Are you really a sailor?" asked Tony.

Old Bill turned toward Tony. "Is water wet? Do birds fly?"

"I understand some ocean liners have beauty salons," said Lucy with a flutter of her false eyelashes. "Is there one on this ship?"

"Yes, lass, I believe there is," replied Old Bill. "This ship is like a floating city. It's got stores, a swimming pool, movies, nightclubs, theaters, anything you want."

"Splendid! I was hoping we'd sail on a ship like this. Can you tell us how to get to the theater?" asked Frederic.

"I was just on my way to the ship's galley," said Old Bill. "The theater is on the way. You can come along if you like."

"What about the kitchen? Is that on the way to the galley too?" asked Tony.

"The galley is the ship's kitchen," said Old Bill, and he looked at each of us, studying our faces. "Any of you are welcome to come along if you've a mind to."

"We've been in that crate for hours," said Vera. "I think we're all hungry."

"Then follow me, mates," said Old Bill, and he leaped up onto one of the crates and started climbing toward the ceiling. Though very old, he climbed with the grace and skill of a much younger mouse.

"Why are we climbing up here? Shouldn't we squeeze under a door somewhere?" asked Tony when we reached the topmost crate.

"No, mate! Through the air ducts . . . that's the

only way to travel on a ship like this," said Old Bill. A few inches above the crate, screwed into the ceiling, was a vent, a metal plate with narrow, rectangular holes in it. "Easy does it," cried Old Bill, and he jumped up, grabbed on to the vent, and pulled himself through to the other side.

Old Bill made the jump to the vent on the ceiling look easy. But we all had trouble following in his paw-steps. Wilbur even slipped and fell the first time he tried it.

The air duct was a long metal tube. Its surface, except for rivets running down its side, was slick.

"I've traveled in air ducts before," said Vera. "They're a good way to get around in large modern buildings."

"What are they for?" asked Tony.

"They bring fresh air to every part of the ship," explained Old Bill, inhaling deeply and casting a wry glance in Lucy's direction. "Smell that salt air? That's the perfume a sailor loves!"

"The smell of food! That's the smell I love," exclaimed Tony.

"I smell food that way," said Wilbur.

"Now there's a lad with a good sniffer!" chuckled Old Bill. "Watch your step and use the rivets to get a good pawhold when we go uphill."

Following the tail in front of us, we set out down the air duct in single file. For the most part we traveled in absolute darkness, but every twenty feet or so we came upon vents cut into the duct. When the vents were open, we were able to catch a glimpse of the cabins beneath. We saw service rooms, storage rooms, work spaces, empty hallways, and private cabins too.

When we came upon a vent that looked down upon a large, cavernous hall with row upon row of seats facing a big red curtain, Frederic exclaimed, "Here it is, Lucy, the ship's theater. Isn't it splendid? Shall we go down and have a look around?"

"But, Frederic, aren't you hungry?" asked Lucy.

"Mice do not live by cheese alone," declared Frederic.

Lucy hesitated. "Well, all right, but then let's get something to eat and pay a visit to the beauty parlor."

"Splendid, whatever pleases your precious fancy, my dear," said Frederic graciously, and he helped Lucy down through the vent onto the curtain. Then, turning to us, he said, "Don't worry, we'll be fine. . . . Meet you back at the crate later on."

As I watched Frederic and Lucy climb down the curtain and hop onto the stage below, a very odd feeling crept over me. "We won't be seeing them back at the crate. We won't be seeing them for a very long time," I thought to myself.

After some time traveling through the air ducts looking down into various cabins as we went along, we came upon the ship's galley. It was a very large kitchen, so large it reminded me of a used-car lot. Instead of cars, stoves and countertops were lined up one right next to the other. The galley was filled with people dressed in white aprons and mushroom-shaped caps. They all seemed very busy.

"Yummm!" said Tony, taking a deep sniff. "It certainly smells delicious down there!"

"I smell a cat!" cautioned Wilbur.

"Can't be, mate, cats aren't allowed in this galley . . . captain's orders," Old Bill assured us.

"Maybe so, but I know what I smell," insisted Wilbur.

"And I know what *I* smell!" exclaimed Tony, and without asking permission, he dropped down through the vent onto some canisters stacked on a high shelf.

"You get back here at once! It's not safe down there!" I squeaked.

"Aw! That's what you always say!" called Tony, and he climbed down onto the countertop toward a bowl of crackers. "See, no cats!" He grinned. "I'll bring up some food in a jiffy."

But as Tony spoke one of the cupboard doors below the counter swung open and a large Siamese cat appeared. Like a spray of water from a garden hose, the cat poured itself through the air. Leaping from the floor, she knocked over the bowl of crackers and lunged for Tony.

(6)

BEHIND TONY WERE TWO LARGE TOASTER OVENS. As the cat loomed up in front of him, Tony jumped into the space between the ovens.

"Johnson! I thought I told you to get rid of that cat!" hollered the head chef, a heavyset man with a pencil-thin mustache.

"Cat? What cat?" said Johnson, turning away from the dishes he was washing.

"Don't try to play dumb with me," screamed the head chef, brandishing his egg whisk. "You know it's against the rules. Now get that animal out of my kitchen or I'm going to report you to the captain."

"But, sir," protested the thin young dishwasher, "I think she's cornered a mouse. See the way she's crouching. She always crouches like that when she's cornered something."

The chef came over to the counter and peered between the toaster ovens.

"Ah yes . . . I can barely make out two beady little eyes. Pesky creatures!" sneered the chef, and stroking the cat with his thick pudgy fingers, he turned on both toaster ovens.

"Good kitty, want a mousie but can't reach it? Don't worry, when it gets too hot, the mousie will have to come out. Then you can have a nice warm meal. Carry on, Johnson."

"Then I can keep Matilda here?" implored the dishwasher. "She hates it in my tiny little cabin."

"Of course," replied the chef. "If she catches mice, she has a job, unless the captain finds out, then you're on your own."

"Thanks, sir!" said Johnson with a smile.

While Johnson went back to his pile of dirty dishes and the head chef continued cooking, Matilda sat poised on the countertop staring at the space between the two toasters. With muscles tensed, ready to spring at a moment's notice, she might easily have been mistaken for a statue.

"People!" fumed Albert. "What creeps! Tony never hurt a hair on their heads, but just because he's a mouse they're going to kill him. And what's his crime? Stealing a cracker? I've seen them in the deli. They *waste* more food than that every ten minutes."

"Our foolish young lad has gotten himself in quite a fix," said Old Bill. "If he was a ship, I'd say he's taking on water."

"I'm going to jump down and divert Matilda's attention," said Vera. "That will give Tony a chance to make a break for it."

"No, wait! I've got a better idea. But there's no time to explain. The rest of you find the captain of this ship and report back here," said Albert, and he set out down the air duct in the direction from which we had come.

"Wait a minute! Come back! What's the big idea?" I ran after him, but Albert is a fast runner. By the time I caught up to him he was lowering himself down through a vent into one of the passenger cabins.

"Would you mind telling me what you're doing?" I called to him.

"Come on down and see for yourself," he replied.

Hooked into the vent was a coat hanger. On the hanger was a cotton smock and below that a bed. I climbed through the vent, grabbed on to the coat hanger, slid down the smock, and dropped myself onto the bed. By this time Albert had leaped onto the small end table next to the bed. On the table was a jar of India ink and a small pad of white paper.

"I saw it on our way to the galley," said Albert as he struggled to get the top off the jar of ink.

"Do you really think that now is a good time to write a letter?" I asked.

"Yes, as a matter of fact I do. Well, don't just stand there—give me a paw."

"But, Albert!" I grabbed hold of the jar of India ink while he screwed the top off. "What does writing a letter have to do with helping Tony?"

"Trust me. Now let's see . . . how shall I begin?" mused Albert, dipping his tail into the ink.

"Albert! This is madness! Our baby brother is about to be eaten by a cat and you're practicing your penmouseship!"

Ignoring me as if I were not there at all, Albert proceeded to write the following letter:

> Dear Captain,
>   I thought you might like to know
>   there's a cat in the galley.
>   A Friend

"There! Now the captain can take care of Matilda," said Albert.

"I get it. You're going to give that note to the captain."

"If we can find him, I will," said Albert, folding the note in half and placing it in his mouth.

As we climbed back up into the air duct I couldn't help but remember Albert's plan to get the watchdog to chase the rats.

"I hope this brilliant idea of yours works better than your last one," I said as we raced back to the galley.

When we arrived, the others were waiting.

"We found the captain, mates. He's on the bridge," Old Bill greeted us.

"How's Matilda?" I asked.

"Same," answered Vera, "but I doubt Tony can hold out much longer."

"Take me to the captain!" cried Albert, and we set out, leaving Vera behind to watch over Tony.

The bridge was a considerable distance from the galley, and there was a lot of steep climbing involved in getting there. As I struggled to keep up the pace I kept thinking of Tony, hoping he could hold out long enough for Albert's plan to work. Finally Old Bill stopped in front of a vent. Huffing and puffing, we gathered around and looked down onto the ship's bridge. Below us we saw a large room with big windows that looked out upon the sea. The room was filled with all kinds of electronic equipment, computers, maps, charts, and radar screens. In the center of the room, directly below our vent, were three men dressed in uniforms. With compass and pushpins in hand, they were bent over a large map.

"The one with the beard is the captain," said Old Bill. "At least I heard the other two call him Captain McCall."

"That's good enough for me," said Albert, and he dropped the note through the vent.

Like a large white butterfly, the note fluttered down and landed on the map just inches from the captain's hand.

"Mmmm, what's this?" he grumbled, squinting as he read the note. "A cat in the galley! Who wrote this?"

The other two men shook their heads.

"Not me," said one.

"Never saw it before," said the other.

"Mmmm, I understand, no one wants to get on the

chef's bad side," said Captain McCall, and picking up the ship's intercom, he rang up the galley. "Hello, this is the captain. Give me the head chef. . . . Hello, Chef? What's this I hear about a cat in the galley? You know it's against the rules. Get it out of there! And, oh yes, have my lunch sent to my cabin at once. I'm hungry! And remember, NO MASHED POTATOES! I *hate* mashed potatoes!"

"It's working!" cried Albert. "But we still don't know if Tony's safe. C'mon!"

Running as fast as our paws could carry us, we raced through the air ducts back to the galley.

"They took Matilda away!" Vera informed us as we approached. "But Tony's still between the two toaster ovens. . . . No, wait! Here he comes!"

Sniffing to make sure the cat was really gone, Tony's head emerged from the shadows between the ovens. He was drenched in perspiration. His eyes looked glazed. His whiskers drooped so low, I was afraid he might trip on them. With shaky steps he slowly edged forward.

"He looks half cooked," said Wilbur.

"Half cooked or not, he'd better scram before the cooks catch him," warned Vera.

"Eleven o'clock and he wants his lunch," complained the head chef, beating the air into a soufflé with his egg whisk. "He's the captain, doesn't he know we're understaffed?"

Meanwhile, Tony looked up at us, smiled, took two steps, and collapsed.

"Tony, get up!" I cried, but Tony didn't move. He

just lay on the counter in plain view, like a wrung-out dishrag.

"Don't let the cooks find you! Hide!" cried Wilbur.

Ever so slowly Tony began to stir. With painstaking effort he raised his head. Then he managed to stand and take a few wobbly, knock-kneed steps. But he was headed in the wrong direction, toward the edge of the counter.

"No don't!" we hollered down to him. "Watch where you're going! Turn around!"

With each faltering step Tony came closer and closer to the edge of the counter. I held my breath.

"If he falls, that'll be the end of him," said Old Bill.

Tony didn't fall. As he came to the edge of the counter he stopped, swayed a little, and turned. For the moment he had avoided disaster, but he was headed down the counter toward the head chef.

"No! Not that way!" we screamed.

We must have made quite a racket. One of the dish-washers stopped what he was doing and looked up in our direction. Oblivious to our calls, Tony continued to plod down the counter, becoming weaker and weaker with every step, until at last he stumbled onto the captain's tray and collapsed in his plate! Lying in a pool of gravy between diced carrots and baked ham, Tony yawned and curled up as if he were going to sleep in his own bed.

"Come on, Vera," cried Old Bill, dropping down through the grate, "we'll keep the cooks busy. The rest of you get Tony out of that plate!"

Scrambling down the canisters, Vera and Old Bill hit the counter running. Albert, Wilbur, and I were right behind them, but while they tore down the middle of the counter, we took cover behind a bag of sugar. Busy with the work of preparing the noonday meal, the cooks didn't notice Old Bill or Vera at all.

Vera knocked a spoon onto the floor.

"Look, more mice!" cried one of the cooks, taking up his spatula as a weapon.

"Get them!" cried another.

While Old Bill and Vera deftly led the cooks on a wild-goose chase, we dashed down the counter onto the captain's plate.

"Come on, Tony." We tried to grab hold of him, but his mind was so befuddled, he pulled away.

"Leave me alone," he moaned. "Can't you see I'm sleeping? Get out of here or I'll squirt you with perfume."

"Oh rats, he's delirious!" cried Wilbur.

Meanwhile, the head chef took a break from chasing Old Bill and Vera just long enough to pick up a stainless-steel metal dome and place it over the captain's tray.

"Oh no!" moaned Wilbur. "Trapped again . . . twice in one day!"

(7)

"JOHNSON, TAKE THAT APRON OFF AND COME HERE."
We heard the muffled voice of the head chef through
the metal dome. "This is Captain McCall's lunch. I
want you to take it to his cabin and—"

"But I'm not a waiter, sir," objected the young dishwasher.

"I said," continued the head chef firmly, "I want you
to take this up to the captain and personally apologize
for having that cat in *my* galley on *his* ship. Understood?"

"Yes, sir!" replied Johnson, and he lifted the captain's tray so quickly, I fell backward into a pile of diced
carrots.

"Phew! That was a close one," said Wilbur. "For a
moment there I thought the head chef saw us."

"No. I've seen them use domes like this one in the
deli," said Albert. "It's to keep the food hot."

The dome was doing its job well. As the atmosphere
beneath it filled up with steam, it got hotter and hotter.

"We've got to wake up Tony and make a run for it as soon as Captain McCall lifts the dome," I said. But Tony was out cold. No matter how hard we shook him, he wouldn't wake up.

"It's not going to work. I've seen pickled herring with more life in them," declared Albert. "I've got a better idea. . . ."

Albert always seemed to have a better idea.

"We'll use the element of surprise. As soon as Captain McCall lifts the dome, I'll throw peas in his face. That will shock him so much, by the time he figures out what to do, you two will have carried Tony to safety."

All this while we heard footsteps; then the footsteps stopped and we heard a knocking sound, like knuckles rapping on a door.

"Your lunch, Captain, sir," said Johnson.

"Come in," answered the captain. As we heard the door open our tray tilted to one side. "Put it on the table."

"Ah . . . err . . ." Johnson stammered, not knowing quite how to begin. "I want to apologize . . . ah, you see it was my cat in the galley and really I'm sorry. It won't happen again. . . ."

"Don't worry about it," replied Captain McCall. "Have you had the cat long?"

"Actually it's not my cat at all," said Johnson. "It's my sister's and I'm watching it for her. I don't even like cats."

"Where's the cat now?" asked the captain.

"I'm keeping it in my cabin," said Johnson, "but it's

a very small cabin and she doesn't like it. Whenever I leave her alone she finds something of mine to sharpen her claws on."

"I happen to like cats. I like them very much," said the captain. "Can't have them in the galley though . . . regulations, you know." The captain paused. "What's your name, sailor?"

"Johnson, sir . . . Larry Johnson."

"Tell you what, Johnson," said the captain. "Why don't you bring that cat up here? And I'll keep it in my cabin for you."

"Really? You mean it? Oh, thank you, Captain!" Johnson was delighted.

"Of course I mean it," said Captain McCall. "I grew up on a farm, you know . . . used to have scads of cats . . . loved every one of them . . . the wilder the better. I'll be on the bridge all this afternoon. Bring her up to me when you come off duty. Do you have Kitty Litter?"

"Yes, sir, and cat food too," replied the grateful dishwasher.

"Good, bring them along," said Captain McCall, "and whatever toys she might own. We want her to be happy, don't we?"

"Yes, sir!" replied Johnson, enthusiastically firing out the word *sir* as if he were shooting it from a gun. "Will there be anything else, sir?"

"No, carry on," said the captain, and Johnson left, closing the door behind him.

"Great! Just what we need, a cat," exclaimed Wilbur.

I shook Tony again. He was still out cold.

"Come on, everybody, get ready. When the captain lifts the dome, I'll start heaving peas," said Albert.

But I had to disagree. "No, Albert, I don't think that will work. Tony's too heavy, and even if we did get away, you'd get caught for sure."

"Well, what do you want to do," squeaked Albert, "just sit here like mashed potatoes?"

"Yes! That's it!" cried Wilbur. "Like mashed potatoes!"

For a moment I thought Wilbur's mind had finally snapped. Then he explained what he meant and I was sure he had gone crazy.

"Look," he said, "we all have white fur. If we sit on our tails, and tuck in our paws and noses, we'll look just like mashed potatoes. And Captain McCall *hates* mashed potatoes. We all heard him say so."

"I have to admit, it's a brilliant idea!" exclaimed Albert. "And it just might work too."

As far as I was concerned, they were both crazy. But there didn't seem to be anything else to do, so I helped Wilbur tuck under Tony's tail. Then I tucked in my own tail and lay down next to Albert.

"Whose whiskers are these?" said Wilbur, scooping some gravy from Captain McCall's baked ham and splashing it on top of us.

"Mine," said Albert.

"Tuck 'em in," said Wilbur. "Mashed potatoes don't have whiskers."

For a few minutes we lay there while the warm gravy slowly oozed into our fur. Then we heard the captain sit down. Pulling the tray closer, he lifted the dome. At that moment I squeezed my eyelids shut and said a very unusual dinner prayer:

Dear God,
Please help us look like mashed potatoes. Amice.

"What's this?" exclaimed Captain McCall in utter outrage. "Mashed potatoes! If I've told that chef once, I've told him a million times, *I hate mashed potatoes!*"

"It's working!" I thought to myself. "Everything is going to be all right." But then the captain sprinkled salt and pepper on his ham. The salt was no problem, but some of the pepper got into my nose and I started to sneeze.

"Ahhh . . . Ahhhhh . . . Ahhhhh," somehow I managed to stifle the urge.

The captain was a fast eater. As he cut up his ham and downed his peas and carrots, we heard his knife and fork clinking against his plate.

"He gobbles his food like Jay does," I thought to myself.

Then I heard the flipping of pages as Captain McCall began to read.

"Good," I thought, "he's reading a book and not

really paying attention to his food. Everything will be fine. Perhaps Wilbur's idea wasn't so crazy after all."

But all of a sudden my body convulsed with three gigantic sneezes.

"Achooo! *Achooo!* ACHOOO!"

My sneezing was so violent, it shook us all and knocked several peas off the captain's plate.

"Mmmm, that's odd," muttered Captain McCall as he nudged us with his fork. "I could have sworn my mashed potatoes just sneezed."

I was sure Tony was a goner, and if we didn't run for it, we'd be killed too. As luck would have it, at that moment the captain's intercom buzzed and he was called away on important business. As soon as we heard the captain's door close, we all jumped up.

"It worked! It really worked!" Wilbur couldn't believe his plan had succeeded.

"Don't let it go to your head, *Sally.* In my book you're still a *pet mouse.* It takes more than brains to make it on the outside—it takes courage!" said Albert.

It was a very unkind remark. Though Wilbur didn't respond, I did.

"Albert," I said, "what are you talking about? Wilbur is as brave as you are any day."

"Oh yeah? Then how come he hid in the pipe when you went into the warehouse?"

"Who told you that?" I demanded to know.

"Vera."

"Forget it, Pearl," said Wilbur. "We've got more important things to worry about right now."

Wilbur was right. This was no time to be arguing. Captain McCall could return at any moment. Tony was still unconscious and there was no way to get him off the table in that condition.

"We'll have to hide somewhere up here until Tony revives," said Wilbur.

The captain's table was cluttered with lots of little things—a box of paper clips, a pencil sharpener, a vase with fake flowers—but there was only one thing big enough to hide in. At the far end of the table, near an open porthole in a wooden cradle, was a large glass bottle. Inside the bottle was a model sailing ship. Made of wood, it had a wide hull and two big sails. Atop its main mast was a black flag with a skull and crossbones.

"It's a model of an old pirate ship!" cried Albert. "Come on! Let's hide Tony in there!"

Grabbing hold of Tony, we dragged him over to the books that were stacked up near the mouth of the bottle. Tony was as limp as raw dough, and we had to struggle to get him into the bottle and onto the deck of the pirate ship.

Delirious, every so often he would cry out, "More French toast, please, do you have any French bread? How about some French fries?"

Opening the hatch, we lowered Tony down a steep narrow ladder and carried him through the mess hall to the crew's quarters. Then we put him in a bunk and covered him with a blanket.

"Tony's in pretty bad shape," said Albert. "We may be here a long while."

"Are you worried about Vera?" I asked.

"Not at all," replied Albert. "That's one mouse that can take care of herself. But I am worried about us. If we're going to be here for more than a day, we ought to stock up on food and water."

"There's a dish of peanuts and a glass of water on the table," I said.

"I saw some buckets on the main deck. We'd better take care of that now, before Captain McCall gets back," said Wilbur.

While Albert and Wilbur went out to get the peanuts and water, I tended to Tony. Until they brought me a bucket of water there wasn't much I could do but hold Tony's paw and stroke his forehead. But once I had the water I found a cup in the pirate ship's galley and got Tony to drink a little. Gently propping him up with a pillow, I held the cup so he could drink. The toaster ovens had dried him out, so the water had an immediate healing effect. In less than an hour his fever was down and he was sleeping calmly.

"Perhaps a nurse is tending to Jay at this very moment," I thought to myself. In my mind's eye I saw her dressed in a white uniform with a white nurse's cap on her head. With all my heart I wished that I could be that nurse and somehow help to make Jay well again. I guess it was a foolish thought for a little white mouse to have, but deep inside I knew my love for Jay wasn't foolish, and it wasn't little either.

"We got all of Captain McCall's peanuts stowed away," said Wilbur, flopping down on the bunk across from Tony, "and several barrels full of water too."

"We also have a plan," said Albert. "It was my idea, but Wilbur figured out some of the details."

"I thought it was my idea," countered Wilbur, "and we figured out the details together."

Albert and Wilbur never did get along very well. Even when we lived in Adams's Pet Store they were never exactly what you'd call best friends.

Their plan was a daring one. They wanted to get the pirate ship out the porthole and into the ocean.

"We'll loop one end of a piece of string around the bottle and tie the other end to Captain McCall's door-knob," said Albert. "When he opens his door—SWOOOSH!—the string will pull us right out the port-hole!"

It was a mad scheme, but after pulling off our mashed-potatoes masquerade, I was willing to consider anything.

"Okay, let's say this string thing works and we get the bottle in the water. How are we going to get the ship out of the bottle?" I asked.

"Haven't you noticed?" said Wilbur, standing up and taking down one of the oil lamps that hung on the wall. "Everything about this ship is very well crafted. There's oil in this lamp, and that mattress and pillow . . . they're made of real straw and goose down."

"We've checked the timbers in the cargo hold. They're solid," said Albert. "Every board from its bow to its stern, every lath and screw, every rope and pulley, and all its sailcloth is accurate and complete down to the tiniest detail."

"But I still say, how are you going to get it out of the bottle?"

"The cannons!" exclaimed Wilbur. "We'll fire the cannons and break the bottle."

"You mean there's real gunpowder on this ship?" I asked.

"Kegs of it"—Albert grinned—"and enough cannon-balls to fight a war."

"But are you sure it's *real* gunpowder?"

Just then Old Bill and Vera burst into the crew's quarters.

"Everyone okay here? How's Tony?" inquired Vera.

"We're fine, and Tony's going to be all right. He just needs some rest. Did the cooks give you much trouble?" I asked.

"Aye, that they did," exclaimed Old Bill. "We had to run through the dining rooms to get away from them—caused quite a stir among some of the passengers. After that we ran down the hall and hid in a closet for a while. Been all around this ship but never to the captain's cabin before. Glad I got around to it, though. He'd got quite a ship here. Not as nice as *Gertrude*, mind you, but quite a ship nonetheless."

"We want to launch her, Bill, but we need someone like you to be our captain," said Albert, and he proceeded to tell Old Bill the plan.

When Albert was finished, Old Bill heaved a deep sigh. "I hate to disappoint you, mates, but my sailin' days are over. I'm retired. Remember?"

"Then you won't help us?" said Wilbur.

"I'll teach you a few things, like how to navigate by the stars—a sparrow taught me that—and I'll show you how to rig the sails and steer, but I can't sail, I'm too old for that."

"What nonsense!" cried Vera. "When we were dodging those cooks in the galley, it was me that had to keep up with *you*, and I'm a pretty fast runner."

"A *very* pretty, fast runner," said Old Bill, with a twinkle in his eye, "but I've paid my dues, I deserve a rest."

"It's *Gertrude*, isn't it?" I said, looking Old Bill straight in the eye. "Deep inside you've made up your mind. If you can't have her, then you don't want any ship. Isn't it so?"

For a moment Old Bill's eyes seemed to catch fire, but then his expression softened.

"We'd be lost out there without a real sailor to help us," said Wilbur.

"It won't be easy, mates, and if I'm to be your captain, you'll all have to follow orders," said Old Bill.

"Then you'll . . ."

"Yes, mates. May *Gertrude* forgive me . . . I'll be your captain," said Old Bill, then, turning his head, he twitched his ears. "Did you hear that?"

Running to the porthole, we looked out through the glass bottle and saw Captain McCall coming in his door. In one arm he held a brown paper bag and a package of Kitty Litter. In the other was Matilda.

(8)

AFTER FEEDING MATILDA THE CAPTAIN DID SOME WORK at his desk. Then he took a shower and got dressed in evening clothes. We watched while he straightened his tie, gave Matilda a gentle pat, and closed the cabin door behind him.

"Looks like he's going to a party or something," said Albert. "That will give us plenty of time to get ready."

"But what about Matilda?" worried Wilbur.

As soon as the captain left Matilda decided to do a little exploring. We watched nervously while she prowled around, sniffing in all the corners. Once she jumped up onto Captain McCall's wicker chair and raked her claws across it, but she never got up on our table. Finally, when she felt satisfied that all was in order, Matilda leaped up onto the captain's bed and settled herself right in the middle of his pillow. Swishing her tail once, twice, three times, she yawned, stretched, and curled up to sleep.

"I don't trust that cat," said Wilbur. "I wouldn't be surprised if she was pretending to sleep just to trick us."

But Albert was confident. "Even if she does wake up, all we have to do is get back to the bottle and we're safe. Come on, there's lots of work to be done."

"Hold on!" exclaimed Old Bill. "Let's wait for a while and make sure the cat is sound asleep before we do anything foolish."

While we waited for Matilda to fall into a deep sleep, Old Bill had us load up the cannons with gunpowder and cannonballs. No one knew exactly what he was doing—how much powder to use or how tight to pack it—but we did the best we could.

"I hope they don't blow up in our faces. I've a mind to go sailing on the water, not through the air," said Old Bill as he rolled a cannonball down the muzzle of one of the big cannons.

When the cannons were loaded, we climbed out of the bottle and down the stack of books onto the table.

Wilbur looked very scared.

"Are you okay?" I asked.

"Yeah, I'm all right," he answered, but the expression on his face was the same one he had had back at the warehouse when he was afraid to go in because of the rats.

Among Matilda's many toys that Johnson had packed in the brown paper bag was a ball of red yarn—the very thing we needed to tie the bottle to the doorknob.

"Listen up, mates," said Old Bill, taking command.

"The first thing we have to do is get the yarn and make a loop around the small end of the bottle."

Matilda's yarn was lying on the floor a few feet from the captain's bed.

"Vera and I will take care of that," said Albert, "but we won't be able to see Matilda once we're on the floor. Give us a squeak if she wakes up. Ready, Vera?"

Vera nodded and they both jumped down onto Captain McCall's wicker chair. From there they climbed down onto the floor. Looking back at us to make sure everything was all right, they pushed Matilda's ball of red yarn over to Captain McCall's table. Then, holding the end of the yarn in their mouths, they climbed up the chair and jumped back to the table.

After threading the yarn through the latch above Captain McCall's porthole, Old Bill tied a loop, which we draped over the neck end of the bottle.

"Are you sure that's the right kind of loop?" worried Albert. "If it doesn't slip off as soon as the bottle flies out the porthole, we're in trouble."

"I think it's the right sort of knot," replied Old Bill, thoughtfully tugging on his gray whiskers. "But then again maybe a clove hitch would work better." And he untied the loop and made another one. This, too, he untied, making a third and eventually a fourth knot.

An hour passed, maybe more, until Old Bill and Albert were satisfied that the bottle was properly rigged. Now we were ready to attach the other end of the yarn to the door.

"I guess Pearl and I will do the honors with the

doorknob," said Wilbur. "Keep an eye on Matilda for us."

As we jumped down onto Captain McCall's chair I said to Wilbur, "Gosh, Wilbur, I never expected you to volunteer for something like this."

"Me neither," said Wilbur, "but all of a sudden the words came out of my mouth. It was like having a hiccup that said something."

"We could still get Vera and Albert to do it," I said. Wilbur looked over at Matilda, then down at the yarn and over to the doorknob, which seemed miles and miles away. For a moment he hesitated. But giving his head a shake, he puffed out his chest. "No, we can do it," he said, and slid down the leg of Captain McCall's chair.

There was plenty of yarn left on Matilda's ball. Leaning back on our hind legs, we gave it a shove. As it rolled across the floor it left a trail of red yarn in its wake.

"I think that's enough, but let's unroll some more to make sure," I said.

Going over to the ball of yarn, we gave it another push. When it stopped we ran over and chewed off what we needed. Our job was already half done. All we had to do now was tie our end of the yarn to the doorknob. Captain McCall's door was made of wood and louvered, so it was not difficult to get a pawhold. Ever so carefully, with the end of the yarn in our mouths, we climbed up to the doorknob.

Holding precariously to the door, we wrapped the

yarn around the doorknob three times and pulled it taut.

"So far so good," sighed Wilbur.

Then Matilda moved. From this height we could see her plainly. Yawning, she stretched and rolled over. Breathlessly we waited for her to go back to sleep again. Then we tied a knot in the yarn so it wouldn't slip when the captain opened the door.

Everything was set. As soon as the door opened, our bottle would be yanked out the porthole.

We hadn't gone very far down the door when Wilbur said, "Smell that?"

At that very moment I heard footsteps coming up the hall. It was Captain McCall. He had had too much to drink and was singing to himself.

"Matilda! Matilda! Take me money and she run Venezuela," he sang loudly over and over again as he stumbled toward his door.

Upon hearing her name, Matilda's ears pricked up, and she roused herself from the captain's pillow. I guess she knew she didn't belong on the bed, for she stood up and jumped down onto the floor.

We had to get back to the bottle before Captain McCall opened the door, but that involved running past Matilda.

"Come on!" cried Wilbur, and we scrambled down the door.

By now Matilda had spotted us. It was like she had a spring coiled up inside of her. As soon as our paws touched the floor the spring let loose and she launched

herself in our direction. But she made a mistake. She hadn't picked which one of us she wanted. While she dived for BOTH of us, we split off in opposite directions, darting deftly around her! By the time she collected herself, we were climbing up Captain McCall's chair. Spinning around, she whipped her body through the air, crashing into the chair with a howl.

"Hey, what's going on in there?" Captain McCall fumbled for his keys.

Matilda had knocked over the chair, but we were already on the captain's table, climbing up into the bottle. As we landed on the deck of the pirate ship, Captain McCall's door swung open and the bottle went sailing out the porthole!

Flung into the night, down, down, down we tumbled until—SPLASH!—we plunged into the ocean.

For a while we spun and turned back and forth and around in the turbulent wake of the ocean liner. Then the great ship passed and we began to gently bob up and down. It was a moment I'll never forget. We were on our way home! I looked at Wilbur and we smiled and rubbed whiskers. As the icy black sea splashed up against the glass bottle, causing the stars to wiggle, I said to Wilbur, "See the stars! Doesn't it look like they're dancing? And you were so brave!"

"I was scared stiff," replied Wilbur.

"So was I," I said, and we both laughed.

"What's wrong with you two?" cried Old Bill, clamoring up the hatch. "Can't you see we're taking on water? We've got to fire the cannons right away!"

Rushing to the railing, we saw what Old Bill was talking about. Every time the mouth of the bottle dipped below the surface of the ocean, water gushed in.

"Fire on command!" said Old Bill, handing each of us a lit wick. We had already decided which of us would fire which cannon. Running on my hind feet with the lit wick in my paws, I hopped up the steps and onto the platform where my cannon was waiting for me.

"Ready, aim," Bill's old but sturdy voice rang out. "Fire!"

BLAM! BLAM! BLAM! BLAM! BLAM! Our cannons rocked back, spitting flashes of fire and clouds of smoke skyward. All at once there was a terrific smashing sound and huge chunks of glass came crashing down. When the smoke cleared, glass littered the deck everywhere. But the ship was sailing free.

"Hurray! We did it!" a cheer rose up.

Coming over to my cannon, Wilbur heaved a deep sigh. "So it was real gunpowder after all. I was worried about that."

"What's the name of this vessel anyway?" said Old Bill, stretching out over the bow. "If we're going to sail her, we ought to know her name. . . . G-O-L-D-E-N H-I-N-D." He read each letter and pronounced the name cautiously. "Golden Hind . . . that's an odd name . . . not as pretty as Gertrude, but I guess it will do."

"There was a real ship called the Golden Hind," said Vera. "I read about it once. She was a famous pirate ship commanded by Sir Francis Drake. Hind is another word for deer. If I remember correctly, Sir Francis named her that because she bounded through the ocean like a graceful deer running through the forest."

"Sir Francis Drake? Was he a duck?" asked Tony suddenly, poking his head up out of the hatchway.

"Tony!" I protested. "You're not strong enough to be up yet. Get back in bed."

"Aww, I'm okay," he insisted. "Where did Frederic and Lucy go? What happened to the ocean liner? Where are we?"

Stepping over the glass, I pointed to the tiny cluster of lights near the horizon. "That's the ocean liner," I said, and proceeded to tell Tony all that had happened since he got trapped between the toaster ovens.

"So Lucy and Frederic are on their way to France," he mused as the last traces of the ocean liner disappeared from view. "Oh well"—he imitated Frederic's dramatic way of talking—"I guess they'll have a *splendid* time."

(9)

OLD BILL REALLY ENJOYED TEACHING US HOW TO SAIL the *Golden Hind.* He showed us how to tie knots, raise and lower the sails, and how to work together to steer and turn the ship. And he showed us how to navigate, using the stars as guideposts. He was a good teacher and never put on airs about being our captain. In the stern of the ship was a very finely decorated cabin reserved for the captain of the ship. In the real *Golden Hind* it was Sir Francis Drake's cabin. It had lace curtains and velvet cushions on all the chairs, a big oak table, a mahogany bed, and beveled mirrors on the wall. But Old Bill never slept there. Instead, he preferred to sleep with the rest of us in the crew's quarters.

There was so much to learn, but Old Bill had a way of explaining things that made everything seem interesting. "Sometimes the wind is like a bull and your sails are like a bull fighter's cape," he said while teaching us how to handle the sails, "and sometimes the wind is like a minnow in the sea and your sail is like a fisherman's net. The more net you throw out, the more minnows you catch, and the faster your ship will go."

"What happens when the bull gets caught in the fisherman's net?" asked Tony. "I mean, do the minnows ever have horns?"

"Indeed they do!" said Old Bill, keeping a serious expression, though the rest of us were all tittering at Tony. "That's why a sailor's got to know his business and always be ready for the unexpected."

It seemed like Wilbur and I had had more than our share of the unexpected lately. Sometimes, when it was my turn to keep watch and mouse the wheel that steered the *Golden Hind,* I daydreamed about Jay and how things used to be. Sometimes I pictured the *Golden Hind* pulling right up to a bathing area on the beach. From the bow of the ship I saw Jay in his bathing suit, making a sand castle. Riding on a big wave, I pictured the *Golden Hind* sailing right into Jay's moat.

"Hi, Jay!" Wilbur and I would call out. "We're back."

Jay would be so happy. He'd take us from the *Golden Hind* and put us in his castle to rule as King and Queen forever.

Almost every night, when the rest of the crew were sound asleep, I'd go up onto the bow, look at the stars, and talk to Jay. I knew he couldn't hear me, but I liked to pretend that I was bouncing my thoughts off the stars to him.

"How are you tonight, Jay?" I'd say. "I hope you're

feeling better and all over the accident by now. We're doing fine. Old Bill said it will take us about a week to get to shore. But I don't know how long it will take to get home. . . . We saw a whale today! At least that's what Tony said it was. He likes to sit up in the crow's nest and look for them. Actually, it looked more like a big gray wave to me. I know you miss us. But you can't guess how much we miss you. Remember the time you had to go visit your grandmother and left us with Billy Chase for a week? I guess he took good care of us. We always had fresh water and plenty to eat. But it wasn't the same as being with you. Oh, he played with us a little, but he didn't have much fun and neither did we. Sometimes I think if it weren't for you, maybe I wouldn't want to be a pet mouse at all. . . . Please get well, Jay. Good night."

It didn't matter much what I said. The important thing was that it made me feel closer to Jay. I missed him so much. Nothing could replace the sound of his voice. Sometimes I thought I heard it in the wind. And I missed the sound of his laughter, too, and the way he cuddled us in his hands and talked to us every night before he went to bed.

Those first few days at sea the weather was very favorable to smooth sailing. All day long the sun shone brightly and the wind blew in a steady northeasterly direction, bulging the ship's sails and pushing her through the sea. All we had to do was steer, and that was easy enough, so we had lots of extra time on our paws.

I especially enjoyed the opportunity to visit with Vera. Vera told me everything about herself and I told her everything about myself. The more we talked, the more we discovered how much we had in common, even though we came from very different backgrounds. Whereas I spent the first part of my life in a pet store, Vera grew up in a shoe factory.

"It was a pretty safe place to live," she told me, "but there wasn't a whole heck of a lot to eat, unless you include shoe leather . . . there was always plenty of that around."

One day we found some needles, thread, and a bolt of cloth in the hold of the ship.

"Let's teach ourselves to sew," said Vera.

"Do you think we really could?" I replied.

Vera was always so positive. "Sure, why not? I remember an old lady who used to come into the deli all the time. She'd sit next to the window with a cup of coffee and sew all day long. She was so old she could hardly keep from spilling the coffee on herself, but she sewed the most beautiful things you ever saw. I watched her sometimes, and it didn't look too difficult. She just kept pushing the needle in and out, and when she got to a corner, she'd turn."

It wasn't quite that easy, but we had fun trying, and somehow I managed to make myself a vest. I have to admit, for the most part our sewing was merely an excuse to be together. The more time we spent with one another, the closer our friendship became. But I often found myself unable to tell Vera everything that was on my mind like I could with Wilbur. For a while it was a real mystery to me. Then I realized what was bothering me and we had a talk.

"Remember the time I told you about Wilbur hiding in a pipe outside the warehouse?" I said.

"Sure, I remember. What about it?"

"Well," I continued, "I thought you understood not to tell anyone else, and yet you told Albert. And you know how he likes to tease Wilbur."

"Oh, I'm so sorry. It was unthoughtful of me," Vera apologized, and I felt she really meant it. "It's just . . . well . . . I didn't think. I hope he doesn't still feel bad about it. I mean everybody loses their nerve once in a while. I certainly do."

"You? Act cowardly?" I exclaimed. "I find that hard to believe."

"Well, it's the truth, a mouse can't afford to be brave *all* the time. We're just not made that way."

After our little talk I felt so much better, and I was able to tell Vera anything that was on my mind.

Tony and Wilbur spent a lot of time with Old Bill. When they weren't helping him with something that had to do with sailing the *Golden Hind*, they were sitting around listening to his endless supply of old sea stories.

Albert was the only one who didn't know what to do with himself. Every day he got grumpier and grumpier, bossing Tony, picking fights with Vera, and making everyone feel stupid. Then one day he called us into the captain's cabin.

"Look what I found!" he cried, holding up an old-fashioned inkpot and reams of blank yellow parchment. "It was at the bottom of this old sea chest. Now I can get to work on my *Mouseifesto* even while we sail."

"But, Albert," said Vera, "you write big with your tail, that paper is too small, and there isn't enough ink in that inkpot to write one sentence that way."

"But look!" Albert grinned. "I found a quill. If I can write with my tail, it won't take me long to figure out how to use this thing."

"Congratulations, mate," chuckled Old Bill. "I expect your having something to do will improve morale on this ship one hundred percent."

In the old sea chest where Albert had found the paper and ink was a black velvet bag. Opening the bag, Tony exclaimed, "Look at this!"

In the bag was a crystal ball.

"Isn't that amazing!" exclaimed Vera. "Sir Francis Drake was said to have had a crystal ball aboard the real *Golden Hind.* The Spaniards said he used it to spy on them to find all the secret hiding places where they buried their treasure. Whoever built this model didn't miss a single detail." Vera was very interested in crystal balls. "You remember Luna, don't you, Pearl?"

"How could I forget Luna?" I replied. Luna is a white cat who belongs to Zelda, a Gypsy fortune-teller. Not only is Luna friendly to mice, but sometimes she "borrows" Zelda's crystal ball to give them helpful "readings."

"I saw Luna a few weeks ago," said Vera. "When she looked into Zelda's crystal ball for me, she said—"

"I know! Don't tell me," interrupted Old Bill. "She said you were going on a long sea voyage."

"Yes. How did you know?" replied Vera, genuinely surprised.

"Well, lass," said Old Bill, twirling his whiskers, "I wasn't born yesterday. I've been around. Seen many a fortune-teller in my day. As I recollect, they always say something like that. . . . And give 'em half a chance, they'll tell you what a famous mouse you were in a former lifetime. If you ask me, they're all in it for the cheese."

Nothing more was said about the crystal ball, but that night, when everyone was asleep, instead of going to the bow of the ship to talk with Jay, I went to the captain's cabin and opened the old sea chest. Reaching into the chest, I picked up the black velvet bag and took out the crystal ball. Then I sat down on the captain's bed and rested the ball on the table.

Like Vera, I, too, believed in crystal balls. Once, some time ago, Luna helped me see things in a different crystal ball. It was a most amazing experience. The things I saw were extremely useful. I wondered now if perhaps I couldn't *see* things in this crystal ball. I even dared to imagine I could see Jay and know how he was doing.

Like pouring water into a pitcher, I poured all my attention into the crystal ball. At first I saw nothing but the yellow-gray-brown grain of the oak table and my own reflection. Toward the center of the ball was a wispy, featherlike flaw. For some reason my attention was drawn to this flaw. As I gazed into the frosty depths of the crystal ball, the flaw seemed to transform itself into a craggy mountain range. It was a lovely sight and I wanted to savor it for a long time. But a milky mist soon filled the valleys and flooded the mountaintops. Once or twice I saw a faint blue light flickering in the distance. Then out of the murky atmosphere I caught a glimpse of white sails, and the stately silhouette of a tall ship came into view. Slicing through choppy waters, it emerged from the mist and drew nearer. A shock of recognition made my whiskers tingle. There was no doubt whatsoever. The ship I was looking at was the *Golden Hind* herself—the real *Golden Hind* of olden times!

As she drew nearer I saw pirates on her deck. Scabbards were hanging from their hips, and they had daggers clenched in their mouths. Like so many venomous spiders, they scaled the ship's rigging and trimmed her sails. They were grim, tattered men with sweaty, hairy chests, tattooed arms, and scarred faces. I was utterly transfixed by the spectacle of it all. Then I saw an even more amazing sight. Standing at the helm of the *Golden Hind* was Sir Francis Drake himself!

Unlike his men, there was no excess of roughness in his looks. His beard and mustache were well-trimmed. His nose was thin and firmly molded. His forehead, high and broad. Only his eyes were fierce and stern.

Drawing still closer, I looked into those eyes and saw

many things. I saw a royal court, a majestic palace, and large white horses pulling a fine carriage. I saw gold goblets and swords with ruby-studded handles, hands counting gold coins, necklaces, bracelets, and expensive brooches. I saw cannons roaring, buccaneers pulling aside other ships, leaping from the yardarm of one ship onto the deck of another. I saw bloodthirsty pirates, daggers flying, innocent women and children screaming in pain. Oh! How I shuddered to see such violence! There was nothing swashbuckling or glamorous about it, but I couldn't take my eyes from the crystal ball.

It was like watching TV. One moment I saw scenes of cruel piracy, then someone or something changed the channel and I saw a treasure chest in a cave. Resting on a pile of gold, it was filled to overflowing with diamonds, precious gems, and jewels. Amid this vision of unbelievable wealth, one gem outshone all the others.

It was a deep green emerald. There were other emeralds in the chest. Some were much larger, but none were brighter. And its color! . . . It was a truly magical and mysterious green, with all the colors of the rainbow somehow contained within it.

Ever so slowly everything began to fade. The vision of the emerald became a blur, a mere slash of green in a pool of pink light. Then gradually a new image emerged. The pink light began to swirl and shift until it formed the outlines of a face. And the slash of green lent itself to the formation of two green eyes. It was the very thing I had hoped for—a vision of Jay.

But he was not well. I don't know how I knew that, but it was painfully clear to me that he had not recovered from the accident. He was alive all right but very ill. He was in some kind of coma, a deep, deep sleep, and he needed my help.

"Hurry! Find the emerald. It will make me well again." Jay's lips didn't move but I heard his thoughts as clear as a bell: "Look behind the picture."

"Jay, are you there? Can you hear me?" I called out, but somehow the spell was broken. In just a few seconds Jay's face faded and disappeared. The vision was over, and all I could see in the crystal ball was that little flaw.

"The picture . . ." I thought to myself. What could he possibly mean? There was only one picture aboard ship and that was of the *Golden Hind* herself.

It hung over the captain's bed. Carefully placing the crystal ball in the velvet bag, I returned it to the cedar chest. Then, standing on the bed, I removed the picture from the wall. Turning the frame over, I pulled out the tiny metal clips that held the picture in place. Suddenly a folded piece of parchment fell to the floor. I picked it up and spread it out on the table. It was very thick parchment yellowed with age. One side was blank. On the other was some kind of map drawn in brown ink.

"Could it be?" My paws began to tremble. "Yes!" I was certain. It was a treasure map!

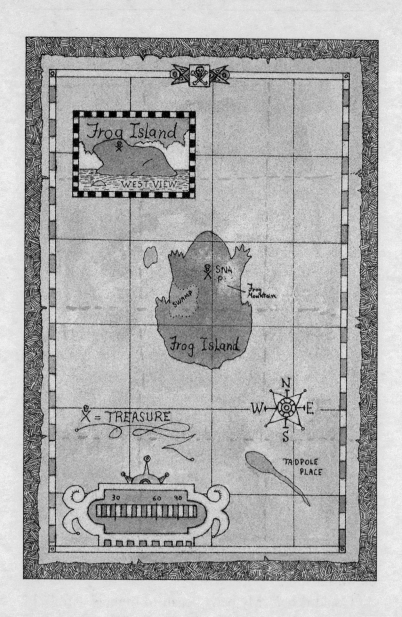

(10)

AFTER I HUNG THE PICTURE OF THE GOLDEN HIND back on the wall above the captain's bed, I went back to my bunk and tucked the map under my pillow. I wanted to wake up Wilbur and tell him the good news. Several times I almost did. I was so excited, I found it difficult to close my eyes. "Pearl," I said to myself, "now that you've found this map, everything is going to be different. In the morning there will be lots to do. You *have* to get some rest." When I awoke everyone was already up and at breakfast. I took the map from under my pillow and ran to the mess hall.

"Look! Look what I found!" I cried, bursting in on everyone.

Pushing aside Tony's bowl of peanut soup, I laid the map out on the breakfast table for all to see. Then I told my story of how I had come to find it.

"Pirates in a crystal ball?" Albert cocked his head to one side coyly. "Treasure map? Come on, Pearl, certainly you don't expect us to believe such a tale?"

"Even a fish would have a hard time swallowing that story hook, line, and sinker," agreed Old Bill. "Must have been a daydream, lass, or perhaps you were sleeping and dreamed the whole thing."

"I wasn't sleeping or daydreaming or anything of the sort!" I protested. "I really did see pirates and I'm sure this map will lead us to Sir Francis Drake's secret treasure."

"I believe in Pearl's pirates!" exclaimed Tony. "And it's got to be a treasure map. See—right here on Frog Island—X marks the spot."

"Anyone can make a map and put an X on it," said Albert. "Besides, what are we, mice or men? Even if we did find treasure, it wouldn't do us a bit of good."

"But Jay needs that emerald!" I insisted. "There's something special about it. I don't know how, but I'm sure it will make him well again. I say we turn this ship around right now and head for Frog Island."

Vera, of course, was very supportive. "I'm with you one hundred percent," she said. "I never met that little boy of yours, but if he means that much to you, I want to help him too."

"Now hold on, lasses." Old Bill raised his paws. "We've plenty of water aboard ship but hardly enough peanuts to get us back to port, so we'll not be going after any treasure on this voyage. As captain, that's my final word!"

"In that case I'll take the dinghy and my share of the supplies and go after the treasure myself!"

"The dinghy's not like the *Golden Hind*, lass. Even a

small squall could swamp her. It would be like sailing a teacup into a tempest," insisted Old Bill.

"Then I'll take a bucket for bailing purposes," I said.

"Well, launch me down the Danube and use my tail for a rudder! If that ain't the darndest thing I ever heard!" exclaimed Old Bill. "Wilbur, my lad, talk to Pearl, maybe she'll listen to you."

"Talk to her? What do you mean? If Pearl's going after the treasure, then I'm going too," said Wilbur, stepping close to my side.

"Can I come?" begged Tony.

"No! I forbid it!" boomed Old Bill. "We're sailing with a skeleton crew as it is. I'll not have three of my sailors jumping ship!"

As quickly as we could, Wilbur and I gathered up our share of the peanuts and water and loaded them into the dinghy. We also took blankets, ropes, knives, needle and thread, and several other items we thought might come in handy. The most important thing, the map, I folded and tucked into the pocket of my vest.

Even as we climbed into the dinghy Old Bill tried to get us to change our minds.

"It's not too late, mates, but it will be soon," he warned.

Slowly we lowered the dinghy down into the water.

"Old Bill's right!" Albert leaned over the railing and called down to us. "Come on back."

"Not until we get the emerald for Jay," I said, and we cast off. Wilbur took the oars and I grabbed hold of the tiller.

"Hope you get lots of treasure!" Tony called down. "I wish I were coming."

Vera said nothing, but as we pulled away I saw her wipe a tear from her eye.

That first day passed slowly. Wilbur and I said little to one another. We just kept rowing. Though we were hungry, we waited until evening to eat. Only then, when the sun went down, did we pull in the oars and lift the lid from our bucket of peanuts.

"We'd better limit the number of peanuts we eat per day," said Wilbur, handing me one. "I think four a day ought to do it."

"Better make it three," I replied.

The sea air was damp and chilled us to the marrow. Wrapping ourselves in blankets, we lay down in the bottom of the boat and ate our dinner. Except for the sound of the sea sloshing against the side of our boat, all was quiet. That night, after Wilbur fell asleep, I took out the map and checked our position against the constellations in the sky. We were on course, but we had a long, long way to go.

"Don't worry"—I looked up at the brightest star in the sky and spoke to Jay as if I were sitting in the palm of his hand—"we'll get that emerald. I promise."

In the morning, when I awoke, I took a turn at rowing while Wilbur moused the tiller.

"I had a dream about Jay last night," said Wilbur, holding on to the tiller with one paw and taking a drink from the water bucket with the other. Wilbur always has lots of dreams and he likes to tell me about them.

"Was I in it?" I asked, also reaching out for a drink.

"As a matter of fact, you were." Wilbur replaced the top on the water bucket. "I dreamed that Jay was a pirate, and we were pirates too. There was a battle and our ship was sinking. You said, 'Let's try the escape hatch,' and all of a sudden we were little birds pecking our way out of an egg. Then Jay started to shiver so we covered him up with our feathers.

" 'Thank you very much,' he said, 'I feel much better now, but do you know what you're going to do next?'

" 'Yes,' I replied. 'I'm going to wake up,' and that's just what I did."

"That's a strange one," I said. "Do you have any idea what it means?"

Wilbur scratched his nose. "None whatsoever."

That day the sea was very choppy. There were even some whitecaps. Once or twice a big wave sloshed over our bow and into the boat. The first time that happened was really scary, but we had no trouble bailing the water out.

Before we went to sleep Wilbur and I had a serious talk and decided to cut our food ration to two peanuts a day. Three peanuts a day, for all the hard physical work we were doing, was hardly enough, and two peanuts left us hungry all the time.

By the fifth day we both had blisters on our paws from rowing. When our spirits lagged, we sang songs like "Row, Row, Row Your Boat" and "How Much Is

That Doggie in the Window?" Sometimes we talked, but most of the time we pulled at the oars, held on to the tiller, and waited for the sun to go down so we could eat.

As we rowed south every day seemed hotter and hotter and lasted longer and longer. On the morning of the sixth day Wilbur told me another one of his dreams:

"I was driving in a car made out of bread," he said, pulling on the oars. "All the trees I passed were made of chopped liver, and the houses were made like log cabins, with celery sticks for the logs and slices of cheese for roofing. I stopped my car and walked into one of the houses. I sat down on a chair made of watermelon rind and nibbled at the tabletop. It tasted like sesame-seed crackers . . . mmmm, it was so delicious! Then I got tired and went into the bedroom. The bed was yellow and shaped like a banana. I peeled down the covers and climbed in. My pillow was made of marshmallows and tuna fish."

"That's it . . . *fish!*" I cried. "There's no need to starve! The ocean is full of fish. Why don't we go fishing?"

"Because we don't have a fishing line or a hook or bait!" said Wilbur. "And even if we did, anything we could catch would probably be ten times bigger than we are."

"Yeah," I sighed, "you're right. I must not be thinking straight. All day long out in the hot sun . . . I guess it's getting to me."

"I know the sun is getting to me," said Wilbur. "It's

starting to look like a fried egg. Sometimes I even think I can hear it sizzling and I can smell it too. You want to hear the rest of my dream?"

"There's more?"

"Lots. I didn't even get to the part where I went swimming in a river of oyster stew—"

Just then I saw something white out of the corner of my eye. As the wave we were on went up, its wave went down. It might have been foam, but I thought it looked like something else. It was several waves over from where we were so I said to Wilbur, "Give me those oars," and started rowing toward it. At first I thought my mind was playing tricks on me. Then I spotted the white thing again.

This time Wilbur did too. "It's a sea gull!" he cried. "Ahoy there!"

(11)

"DON'T GET TOO CLOSE," CAUTIONED WILBUR AS WE rowed nearer. "It may be dangerous."

"I beg your pardon! But I'm a *she* not an *it.* Dora's my name," said the sea gull in a lovely but weak voice. "And I don't think I could hurt you even if I wanted to. I'm almost gone now . . . a basket case to be sea-sure. . . . A tisket, a tasket, a white and yellow basket . . . I've lost my basket with me inside. . . ."

Rowing still nearer, it was plain to see that Dora was not well. Her feathers were wet, her eyes, bloodshot and droopy.

"Is your wing broken? Can't you fly?" I asked.

"My wings are fine," replied Dora, stretching out her great white wings for us to see. "Fishermen . . . that's my problem . . . fishermen and string."

"I don't understand. There are no fishermen around here, nor any string for that matter," said Wilbur, and he whispered to me, "Maybe she's not a sea gull after all, maybe she's a loon."

"I heard that!" snapped Dora. "You think I'm crazy, don't you? Well, perhaps I am, and you would be too—three or four, five, six, seven times as crazy as me if your feet were all tangled up in fishing line."

"I'm sorry, Dora," I said. "We'd like to help you if we can, but we don't understand what you're talking about."

"Fishing line!" squawked Dora. "My feet are all tangled up in it and there's something heavy on the other end, so heavy it's weighing me down, down, down, like a clown on the ground, so I can't fly. That's why I don't even know what it is, 'tis, whiz—but I dream about it—a hook stuck in seaweed? An apple made of lead, a baby carriage with a turtle inside, a turtle with a baby carriage inside, who knows? It could be anything. It could be an old boot, a radio, a box of nails, but I think it's seaweed. I swam into it when I was in shallow water. Then the tide went out and I can't get loose. For days now . . . in a haze now. It seems like a lifetime . . . I've been drifting out to sea . . . drifting, drifting, drifting, and sometimes I think I'm flying and the water is air, and it's mud, too, and I can see a great nest in the sky, perched in a cloud that looks like a tree . . . or is it perched in a tree that looks like a cloud? I can never tell. Oh well . . . drifting, drifting, drifting . . ."

Dora suddenly paused and cocked her head to one side. "Oh, goodness me! Have I been talking nonsense again? I've been out here so long all by myself, you can't imagine how lonely and frightening it's been, and

I'm afraid I've lost my mind"—Dora giggled—"lost my mind in an orange rind . . . been so unkind, can't find what's mine, oh be my valentine . . . maybe it's a sign?"

"Don't worry, we understand the problem now," I told her.

"That's all we need—a flaky sea gull," mumbled Wilbur, but I don't think Dora heard him.

"Maybe we can help you," I said, reaching down to the bottom of the boat for the two small daggers we had packed away in case of emergency. My intention was to use the knives to help Dora, but as soon as she saw them she recoiled in fear.

"Yes! That's it, death, the final cure!" she cried. "But I'm not prepared to die. To answer the question why with truth and not a lie. Please, don't kill me!"

"No, no, you've got it all wrong. I wasn't thinking of *that*," I reassured her.

"Then what were you thinking of? That knife looks sharp, I'm not ready to play a harp," said Dora.

"I want to make a deal," I said. "We'll dive down and cut you loose, but first you must promise to bring us some fish in return."

"Promise . . . yes, I promise," replied Dora. "I primrose promise. Like the sun that drips and the rain that shines, I promise from the start with all my heart, really I do . . . but, boo hoo! It can't be done, though it may be fun, I can't even lift my feet out of the water. Whatever's down there is so heavy, heavy heavy heavy, down at the levee, heavy cream, milk and sugar—"

"Okay, okay!" I cut her off. "You're losing it again, Dora. Just keep still and we'll dive down and cut the fishing lines."

Poor Dora. Sometimes she seemed quite sane. But even when she was acting crazy I kind of liked her.

Taking one of the daggers, Wilbur said, "Let me go first," and he tied a length of rope around his waist. "Hold on to this," he said, giving me the other end of the rope.

"Do be careful."

Clasping the dagger between his teeth, Wilbur stood up and dived down into the sea. When the splash cleared, all I saw was his tail. Then that, too, disappeared beneath Dora's breast.

"He-he-he!" Dora cried. "That tickles!"

Soon Wilbur reappeared, gasping for breath. Reaching up, he held on to the side of the boat.

"What a tangle it is down there!" he said, panting like a dog on a hot summer day. "Sheer spaghetti! I can hardly see your feet amid all the string!"

"String, thing, fling!" cried Dora. "Your ears are wet and much too small, you'll never fly with ears at all!"

Wilbur gave me a pained look, as if to say "Is this really worth it?"

"You want me to dive?" I asked.

"No." Wilbur shook his head. "Just tell her to keep her feet still."

"I'd like to see him keep his feet still when someone was tickling them," muttered Dora with a grimace.

While I held the rope, Wilbur made two more dives.

Everything was going fine. Coming up for air after the third dive, Wilbur announced, "One foot's almost free."

"Thank heaven, times seven, makes eleven!" cried Dora.

"Want me to take a turn now?" I asked.

"No need," said Wilbur, and down he went again.

But this time something went wrong. I felt a pull on the rope. Then it went slack. I tugged and felt nothing. I pulled some more until finally I pulled the rope right out of the water!

"Hold on to our boat with your beak," I told Dora, whipped off my vest, and, clenching my dagger between my teeth, dived overboard.

As soon as I hit the water I started kicking and propelled myself beneath Dora. There was Wilbur, all tangled up in Dora's fishing line. In his frenzied effort to free himself, he had cut his own safety line.

"Wilbur!" I called out, air bubbles escaping from my mouth.

Wilbur saw me and the panic disappeared from his eyes.

Together we hacked away at the fishing line until Dora's feet were free. But Wilbur was still ensnarled in the string. Like some watery elevator cut loose from its cables, the weight at the other end yanked him downward. It would have been easy for me to let go, but I held on.

Wielding our daggers, we hacked away at the octopuslike string. More than once we came within a

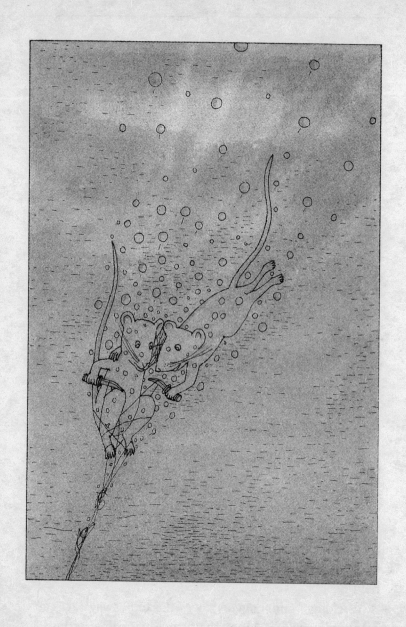

whisker's breadth of cutting one another. Already our air supply was low. Finally there was but one loop of string to cut. I slipped my dagger through, pulled, and Wilbur was free.

Holding on to each other, we kicked and clawed our way toward the sun, which shone like a golden prize above us. My lungs were nearly empty now. My muscles ached. It seemed like we'd never get there, but at last we reached the top.

"Air! Air!" gasped Wilbur.

For several long minutes it took whatever strength we had merely to hold on to the side of the dinghy. Then we pulled ourselves aboard, collapsing in a pile. Even when our breathing was back to normal we didn't move for some time. All we could do was lie there staring into each other's eyes, glad to be alive.

I looked up. There was Dora flying high above us. Dipping low, she soared past and called down, "Thanks, cranks, ranks, banks!" She squawked and then, flapping her wings, caught a sea breeze that carried her high and far away.

Dora never returned with our fish. Perhaps it was foolish of me to think that she ever would. She was crazy. There was no denying it. But something made me trust her.

All that day and the next the sea and Wilbur grew more and more choppy and turbulent. While I bailed, Wilbur rowed. Pulling at the oars with each stroke, he muttered, "Ocean, ocean, ocean."

We no longer had the strength to talk or cheer ourselves up with songs. When it was my turn to row, I
grabbed hold of the oars. My paws were so weak and
blistered, it hurt merely to hold them.

Lifting the lid to the food barrel, Wilbur said, "Two
peanuts left."

"Let's have them now," I said.

Wilbur reached into the barrel and took out the two
peanuts. One of them was quite a bit smaller than the
other.

"Here, you take the big one," he said.

When I refused, Wilbur's temper flared. He shot up,
nearly capsizing the boat. "Take it!" he said, and he
threw the peanut at me. "And take this one too!"

"Wilbur"—my voice trembled—"please don't talk
to me like that . . . not now."

Wilbur sat down and buried his head in his paws.

"I'm sorry, Pearl," he said meekly. "I just wish we
hadn't done this."

"We did it for Jay," I said, reaching out and touching
him on the shoulder.

Then Wilbur looked up at me. His eyes were soft
and sad.

"You did it for Jay," he said.

"What do you mean?" I asked. "Don't you care
about Jay?"

"Of course I do," snapped Wilbur, "but not enough
to throw away my life like this!" Wilbur paused to look
out at the sea. Then he turned to me. "I did it for you,
Pearl."

For what seemed like a long time, but was probably no more than a minute or so, Wilbur was silent. When he spoke his voice was shaky.

"I have a confession to make," he said. "I've been thinking about not going back to Jay. That is if we ever get out of this alive."

I was utterly stunned. Though I heard Wilbur's words, it took a while for the meaning to sink in.

"Not go back? . . . Where would we go? What would we do?" I asked.

"We'd throw in with Old Bill and Tony," said Wilbur. "They're going to sail around the world! Old Bill told me all about it. He likes the *Golden Hind* almost as much as *Gertrude*. He wants to travel again and he wants us for his crew. I always thought I had to be a pet mouse, but I don't. I've got brains *and* courage. I can make it anywhere!"

Splitting the peanuts in two, I kept one small and one large half for myself. The other two halves I gave to Wilbur. Wilbur took his share, wiped a tear from his eye, and we ate.

"What if I did go with Old Bill, would you come with me or go back to Jay?" asked Wilbur as he slowly munched his share.

"That's not a fair question," I protested.

"But I need to know," insisted Wilbur.

"We're in a difficult situation," I said. "You're tired and scared and so am I. Let's not talk about it now."

"Come on, Pearl, answer the question. If I went sailing with Old Bill and Tony, would you come with me or go back to Jay alone?" Sometimes Wilbur can be unbearably persistent.

"Please, Wilbur, I can't answer that question. . . . I just don't know what I would do."

Having finished his peanut, Wilbur slid down into the bottom of the boat. "Well, I guess it doesn't matter anyway," he mumbled, and fell asleep.

We had reached the bottom of the barrel and our future looked grim. In the morning, before the sun was up, the ocean splashed water in our faces. A big storm was brewing. The darkening sky above us looked as if someone were pouring ink into the clouds. The wind began to whip up the sea. It sent huge waves like marching columns of soldiers toward us.

"Good news!" said Wilbur. "Looks like we're not going to starve to death after all. Looks like we're going to drown. I'd much rather drown, wouldn't you?"

"Haven't thought much about it." I had to raise my voice to be heard, for the wind was growing louder.

All at once there was a flash of lightning, a crack of thunder, and water began pouring into the boat from the sky as well as the ocean. For a while we attempted to bail, but it was hopeless. As soon as we got rid of one pail of water, ten more took its place.

The wind howled, shrieking like a wild animal.

Then a gigantic wave swamped us. The boat capsized and we tumbled into the sea.

Though we managed to grab hold of the dinghy, we knew our luck had run out.

"I guess this is it!" I hollered above the raging storm. "Good-bye, Wilbur! I . . . I . . . love you."

"Good-bye, Pearl," cried Wilbur. "I love you too. Maybe we'll get to share a cage in heaven."

"I don't think there are any cages in heaven," I called, "but if there are, I hope we get to share one together."

I was certain that this was the end, but just as the dinghy was wrenched from our grasp and we slipped into the water beneath the crest of a huge wave, I heard Old Bill's voice call out, "There they are!"

(12)

At first I thought it was some trick of the howl-ing wind. Then I turned and saw the hull of the *Golden Hind* splashing through a mountainous wave.

"Here, grab hold of this," hollered Old Bill, and he threw a line down to us.

As the ship's bow plunged into the sea Wilbur and I grabbed hold of the line. Riding up on the next wave, the *Golden Hind* yanked us part of the way out of the water. Then Old Bill, Albert, and the others, hauling paw over paw, quickly pulled us up and over the ship's rail. Drenched to the bone and shivering, I fell against Old Bill and gave him a hug.

"That'll be enough of that, lass," grumbled Old Bill. "Get below deck and warm up before you catch pneu-monia."

The sea was playing catch with the ship, tossing her from wave to wave. Opening the hatch, a surge of water propelled us down the stairs.

"We'd better help the crew," cried Wilbur.

"No, Old Bill said to put both of you in a dry bunk," insisted Vera, "and that's just what I'm going to do."

Wilbur and I were too exhausted to argue. As soon as we dried off we climbed into our bunks, pulled our blankets up over our heads, and fell fast asleep.

When I awoke it was midmorning of the next day and the *Golden Hind* was sailing on a calm sea. Sitting up in my bunk, I looked out the porthole. The sky was like a big friendly blue face.

Quietly climbing out of my bunk so as not to awaken Wilbur, I tiptoed into the mess hall. There I met Vera, sitting at the table.

"So you're up," said Vera with a smile. "How are you feeling?"

"Embarrassed," I answered. "First chance I get, I'm going to apologize to everyone."

"Not at all," exclaimed Vera. "If anything, we owe *you* an apology. Let me get you something to eat. That ought to explain a lot in itself."

As far as I was concerned, Vera was talking in riddles. But when she returned from the galley with a bowl of *fish* soup, I was really confused.

"Where did you get this?" I asked.

"From a sea gull by the name of Dora," replied Vera with a grin. "The wackiest bird I ever met. She simply dropped out of the sky one day with a fish in her beak. She said it was for us because two white mice had saved her life. In between a lot of rhyming nonsense talk she

told us how you and Wilbur rescued her from certain death."

"We did," I said, downing a big delicious spoonful of fish soup, "and she was supposed to help us out in return."

"That's what she said," Vera continued, "and she wanted us to tell you if we ever saw you again that she was sorry. She said to tell you that her mind was so mixed up, she didn't know what she was doing. By the time she came to her senses she couldn't find you again. Actually she was still pretty wacko . . . but she gave us the fish and that's what saved us. We were down to our last peanut with no land in sight. If it hadn't been for that fish, we wouldn't have made it. After we got it all cut up and stored in barrels with seawater, Old Bill turned the ship toward Frog Island. And why not? We've got plenty of food now."

"What happened to Dora?" I asked.

"Oh, she flew off 'to dance with the clouds,'" said Vera.

Good old Dora. I'd love to meet up with her again, if only to thank her.

In the days that followed, Wilbur and I got lots of rest and ate plenty of fish soup. I was soon completely recovered, and except for a slight cold, so was Wilbur. Even our blisters went away. It was good to be aboard the *Golden Hind* again. And best of all, Old Bill insisted on taking us to Frog Island!

"If it hadn't been for your foolish escapades, lass," he

declared loudly, "we would have starved to death. It's the least we can do to take you to Frog Island."

Tony was delighted, and Vera was pleased too. Only Albert grumbled.

"If there's a Frog Island, then I'm a green mouse!" he said again and again.

For a while it looked like Albert was right. A week passed and then another. We had plenty of food, but our water supply was starting to run low.

Old Bill and Albert managed to save the dinghy. They pulled it out of the stormy sea and lashed it down. Everything that was in it was lost. Luckily I had the map in my vest. One day I was sitting on my bunk studying it when Wilbur sat down beside me.

"I was just talking to Old Bill," he said. "We've been sailing for some time now and he says we should have sighted Frog Island days ago. I'm beginning to think maybe Albert is right and there is no Frog Island."

"So you want to give up and go sailing around the world with Old Bill? Is that what you want?"

"Well—er—" Wilbur stammered, "I just think we ought to—"

Just then we heard Tony call down from the crow's nest, "Albert's a green mouse!"

I folded the map, stuck it in my vest, and raced up to the main deck. Old Bill was leaning over the rail peering through his spyglass.

"By jingo, there she blows!" he chortled, and handed me his spyglass. "Here, Pearl, have a look-see."

With the naked eye Frog Island looked like nothing

more than a tiny purple-green bump on the horizon. But with the spyglass I was able to see its distinctive froglike silhouette. Everyone was so excited. Even Albert wanted to look through the spyglass. But Old Bill insisted we had work to do.

"Hop to!" He snatched the spyglass away from Albert. "We'll have to bring her about. Get ready to weigh anchor!"

Old Bill knew exactly what he was doing. With great skill and care he guided our every move, steering the *Golden Hind* toward Frog Island. The closer we came, the more it looked like an enormous frog.

"Gosh, it looks like it might flick out its tongue any moment and snatch a cloud from the sky," declared Tony. "We'd better land fast before it decides to hop into the water."

Avoiding a direct assault, Old Bill wisely maneuvered the *Golden Hind* into a lagoon created by the frog's front feet. Here, in this protected spot where the water was calm, we weighed anchor and made preparations to go ashore.

While I helped load up the dinghy with needed supplies, I couldn't help remembering those difficult days that Wilbur and I had spent in it. Wilbur hadn't said anything more about not going back to Jay. In fact, we both carefully avoided the subject. But it was always in the back of my mind. Sometimes during the winter, when Jay was away at school all day, it got pretty boring in our cage. So I understood why Wilbur was attracted to the whole idea of throwing in with Old Bill. Heck, I wouldn't mind sailing around the world. Who wouldn't? But not going back to Jay—that was another matter. As far as I'm concerned, he's my boy as much as I'm his mouse. But what if Wilbur wanted to go without me? How could I choose between Wilbur and Jay? It would be like trying to decide whether I want to breathe or eat.

When our gear was packed, everyone climbed into the dinghy, everyone, that is, but Old Bill.

"I'll be staying with the *Golden Hind*," he said. "Someone's got to keep an eye on her. If the weather changes, I may have to pull up anchor, but don't worry, mates, when you get back we'll be here." I think Old Bill could have come with us if he'd wanted to, but as he often said, *"Gertrude,* forgive me, but I've grown attached to this new ship like a barnacle!" No doubt he was worried that something bad might happen to the *Golden Hind* in his absence, and he wasn't about to lose another ship that he loved.

The water in the lagoon was as calm as a puddle, and we had no trouble beaching the dinghy. It was strange not to feel the pitch and yaw of the sea as we stepped out onto the sandy beach of Frog Island. We had been at sea so long, standing on firm ground felt odd.

When all our supplies were piled on the beach, we dragged the dinghy farther ashore and hid it under some wide leafy plants.

"Gosh, it looks like a real jungle in there," said Tony with a tremor in his voice as he peered into the dense undergrowth that lay beyond the beach. "There could be *all sorts* of animals in there."

Unfolding the map, we checked our position against the compass.

"I think we're here," said Wilbur, pointing to a spot on the map, "which means that must be Frog Mountain."

"Look here by the *X*," said Vera, pointing to the spot on the map where the treasure is supposed to be. "What's this *SNA* and *P* mean?"

"I've been wondering about that," I replied. "I think there were some other letters there once."

"Yes," agreed Albert, "it looks like water stained them away."

"Could it be *SNAP* and *POP?*" guessed Tony.

"We'll soon find out," said Wilbur, folding up the map and handing it to me. "Let's divide up the supplies and get a move on. The sooner we get this treasure and get back on the *Golden Hind* the better I'll feel."

In a little while we were all set to go. I had the map, a compass, and a length of rope to carry. Everyone else carried something too. Leaving the beach behind, we set out into the dense jungle. The air was hot and damp and full of rich exotic smells. The ground was covered with rotten wood, soft green mosses, and giant mushrooms. Tall stalks, wide leafy ferns, meandering vines, and giant trees arched overhead. Once in the jungle we found that very little sunlight penetrated down to our level. But everywhere we looked we saw lovely bright pink, purple, and yellow flowers.

"I wish I didn't have a cold," said Wilbur, sticking his head inside a large yellow blossom. "I can't smell this flower at all."

Albert gave the flower a sniff.

"That's because it doesn't have any smell."

"It may not have any scent," said Vera, stroking its slender blossom, "but it's the most unusual flower I've ever seen."

"If you think that flower is odd," said Tony, pointing to the squat tubular plant he was standing next to, "listen to this one . . . it talks."

"Ha-ha, very funny," said Albert mockingly.

"No, really, I mean it," said Tony. "Put your ear up close and you can hear it."

"Tony, plants cannot talk," said Albert in an annoyed tone of voice, "and I don't think any of us are in the mood to fool around with nonsense of that sort."

"Oh, Mouse!" cried Wilbur, putting his ear up against the plant Tony was talking about. "I believe this plant *is* trying to tell us something."

"Can't be!" said Albert, also stepping closer to listen. "Wait a minute. I think I hear something."

"I told you," said Tony.

Vera and I put our ears up against the plant.

"I don't hear a thing," said Vera. Then something in the plant moved and I heard a muffled voice.

"Help! Me want out!" the plant cried.

"Did you hear that?" exclaimed Tony.

"You bet I did!" cried Vera.

"This plant wants to leave the jungle," said Tony.

"Maybe it's not getting enough sunlight here. We should dig it up and take it with us."

Again a voice from within the plant cried out. This time its call was even louder:

"Help!"

"Don't worry, old plant"—Tony patted its thick green stem—"we'll do our best. I only hope your roots don't go down too deep."

"Stand back, I'm going to cut it open," announced Wilbur, pulling out his dagger.

"No! Don't hurt the talking plant!" cried Tony, and he tried to stop Wilbur.

"But, Tony, you don't understand," said Wilbur, and he shoved Tony aside, raised his knife, and cut a long slit down one side of the plant. As Wilbur's blade sliced through the fleshy pulp and a white sappy fluid poured forth, Tony screamed:

"Murderer!"

Tony was about to leap on Wilbur's back and pull him from the plant. But as he readied himself to spring, whiskers and a brown nose popped out of the slit.

Dropping his knife, Wilbur reached into the plant and pulled out a tiny brown mouse.

Gasping for breath, the mouse lay on the jungle floor.

"Holy Swiss cheese!" gasped Albert. "I wouldn't believe it if I didn't see it with my own eyes!"

Nearby some low-growing blue flowers had collected tiny pools of rainwater in their blossoms. Taking these blossoms in her paws, Vera dumped some water on the young mouse. This revived him enough so that he was able to sit up and tell us what happened.

"My name Wamba," he said with a grateful smile. "I walk in jungle. I play. I hide from Momma. She collect juba nuts for dinner. I have fun. Momma tell Wamba not go near meat-eating plants. I not see. Plant grab Wamba. Hear Momma call. I call Momma. Momma not hear!"

Tony shook his head. "And I thought the plant was talking."

"How long have you been in the plant?" I asked Wamba.

"Long time," replied the young mouse. "Momma look and look but not find Wamba."

"Could you find your way home from here?" asked Albert.

"Yes," replied Wamba, and he stood up. "Wamba show. You follow?"

"We'd better go with him," said Vera, "and make sure he gets home safely."

So Wamba led the way to his village and we followed.

"Not far, village beyond stream," said Wamba.

A few minutes later we came upon the stream Wamba had mentioned. It was a tiny trickle of fresh spring water. Wading through it was no problem. On the other side we found ourselves in a village of grass huts.

(13)

As soon as we entered the village we were surrounded by native mice.

"Wamba back!" the call rang out. "Wamba found."

Bursting out of the largest hut, located in the center of the village, Wamba's mother ran to his side. Though her first words were reproachful ones, the tears running down her cheeks were tears of joy.

"Never, never run away again!" she scolded. "Where you go?"

"I not go anywhere. I play. Meat-eating plant snatch Wamba. I afraid . . . I call and call and call. Then good mice find Wamba."

Wamba's mother, Lowpa, treated us very graciously, and his father, Boorha, who was chief of the entire tribe, insisted that we remain long enough to be properly honored for the good deed we had performed.

"We dance and celebrate. Wamba found. We give thanks to you and spirits that guide you here."

I was just about to tell Boorha that we could not accept his invitation to stay when Albert whispered to me, "It's probably not wise to refuse their hospitality," and he turned to Boorha:

"We will gladly stay to celebrate your good fortune, but then we must leave to climb yonder mountain."

At the mention of our climbing Frog Mountain, Boorha's pleasant expression changed to one of extreme concern. For a moment it looked like he was going to warn us about something. But he stopped himself and, turning to the villagers, said solemnly:

"Let drummers beat rhythm of joy and celebration, and dancers' paws thump out all sadness in dust. Let jungle spirits hear our songs and know that we are grateful."

At these words the whole village burst into a flurry of activity. Many mice rushed into their huts, only to reappear wearing the most fantastic costumes. They wore long grass skirts, masks made of bark painted with berry juice and mud, and elaborate headdresses.

Soon half the villagers were dancing in a circle around the main hut while twenty or more mice pounded on large drums made of seaweed stretched tightly over snail and clam shells. It was a joyous spectacle, a rare treat to behold. The drumming was both hypnotic and lively, and the dancers never missed a single beat. Swinging their tails, they jumped and leaped over one another, tumbling over the jungle floor like acrobats in a circus. Young and old alike, they

danced with wild frenzy and abandon, and sometimes their antics made everyone laugh.

The atmosphere of fun was infectious, so much so that we had to restrain Tony to keep him from joining in. For we were the honored guests, and it was not considered proper that we should be a part of the celebration. Someone, after all, had to be the audience, and we were it.

With great ceremony we were led to the main hut in the center of the village. There, with Boorha, Lowpa, and Wamba, we were seated on seedpod pillows and served all the tasty delicacies that the jungle could provide. This was by no means a meager feast. Until that day I would never have believed that so many new tastes could exist!

The celebration lasted all afternoon and well into the evening. The dancers never seemed to tire. When the sun went down, they rested a little, but only until the moon came up. Then with renewed vigor they began to dance again.

"Each dance tell story," explained Boorha. "Each story tell history of tribe. Ours long story, many adventures, much wisdom gained. Dance now tell of mountain and monsters that live there."

Some of the dancers had donned ferocious-looking masks. While others mimed climbing a mountain, those dressed like monsters lay flat on the ground as if hiding. When the climbers reached the top of the mountain, the monsters rushed out and attacked them.

The climbers tried to fight back, but the monsters vanquished them and danced over their corpses.

"This dance, old dance, given to tribe for reason. Wise mouse learn much from ancestors . . . avoid trouble . . . save sorrow."

"Have you ever climbed Frog Mountain and seen the monsters with your own eyes?" asked Albert.

"No, not father, not his father, not great-great-grandfather set paw on mountain."

"We're not afraid of anything," declared Tony.

"Anything?" I asked Tony.

"Well, almost anything," he corrected himself.

"Not matter of fear," replied Boorha patiently. "Boorha face fear when need to, but sometimes better to walk in pawprints and follow tails of wise ancestors."

"But we *have* to climb the mountain," I said, "that's what we came here for. Besides, the monsters in your dance lived a long time ago, chances are they've died out by now. . . ."

"Then you go up mountain." Boorha nodded thoughtfully, and with a single clap of his paws all the dancing and drumming came to a sudden halt. "We give thanks, now we rest," he said to the villagers, and bowed to them in a ceremonial manner. After bowing in response, every member of the village stretched up on their hind legs and waved their paws in the air.

"Long live Boorha!" they cheered three times, and the celebration ended almost as quickly as it had begun.

"You tired, no?" said Lowpa. "Come, take to hut, you rest."

The visitor's hut looked no different than any of the other huts. Constructed of straw tied together with thin strands of grass, it had one main door that faced the center of the village. There were no windows. The floor was covered with woven mats, which kept us off the damp ground.

In the morning we washed in the stream. Then we were taken to Boorha's hut and given a huge breakfast. There was so much food, we couldn't finish half of what was given.

"I almost feel like I'm back in the deli," commented Vera with a dainty burp. "Do you eat this richly all the time?"

"Jungle provide. We eat well," replied Boorha.

When it came time to leave, we stood up and thanked our hosts, but Boorha would not let us leave alone.

"It not right honor guests one night, send to doom next morning. If you must go up mountain, I pick strongest mice. You go. We go with you."

It was a brave gesture on Boorha's part. Though we tried to change his mind, he could not be convinced to let us go alone.

"If monsters dead, we find out. That good," he argued. "If monsters alive, you need help. Both ways, it good we go."

"Wamba come? Yes, Poppa?" asked Wamba.

"Wamba not come!" said Boorha. "Wamba too young!"

Tony was disappointed that his new friend, Wamba, was forbidden to accompany us up the mountain.

"You can stay in the village and play with Wamba. We'll pick you up on the way back," I said to Tony.

"And miss finding pirate treasure? Not a chance!" exclaimed Tony.

Well-fed and rested, we set off into the jungle again toward Frog Mountain. Boorha insisted that his mice help carry our supplies. With their help and expert guidance we found that we were able to travel twice as fast through the jungle as we had the day before.

Today the jungle was even hotter. As the morning wore on it got so hot, I took my vest off and put the map in one of the chests we had brought along. Planning to pick my vest up on the way down the mountain, I hung it on a bamboo shoot.

"We rest here," said Boorha. "It long climb up mountain."

When rainwater could not be found in the hollow parts of plants, Boorha knew just which stems were juicy enough to chew. Around noon we reached the base of Frog Mountain and began to climb. At first the slopes were gentle and the footing was firm. But before long we met with some rough going. Easy paths veered almost straight upward and we had to proceed very slowly. More than once some large pebbles and stones were dislodged, causing minor landslides. Luckily no one was hurt and the climb continued.

Once, when I stopped to check the map, Boorha

said, "You have many strange things. From what plant you take this bark?"

"It's not really bark, but it is made from trees," I told him. "It's called *paper.*"

"Why you keep stopping? Why always look at *paper?*" he asked.

"It tells me where to go," I replied.

Boorha put his ear next to the map. "I not hear anything. This *paper*—it speaks to your ears but Boorha not hear."

Apparently Boorha's tribe had not yet discovered the art of reading and writing, so I said, "This paper does not speak to my ears but to my eyes." Boorha nodded as if he understood.

As we climbed I often looked down at the lovely view. Beneath the lush jungle hillside I could see the beach below. From this high vantage point it appeared to be a mere yellow line surrounded by a vast, sparkling blue sea.

"You live in a beautiful place," I said to Boorha.

"Beautiful, yes," he replied. "It speaks to Boorha's eyes, heart, and soul."

It was late afternoon when we scaled the last steep precipice and pulled ourselves over the topmost ridge of Frog Mountain. Even Boorha seemed exhausted, but weary as he was when he reached the summit, he jumped up and down and started hollering at the top of his lungs.

"I say, not come! Not come!" he cried again and again.

At first I couldn't tell who he was hollering at. Then I saw Wamba.

"But I not baby. Wamba brave like Boorha."

Boorha took a deep breath and patted Wamba on the head. "It no good send home now. How you get here so quick?"

"Wamba take shortcut through swamp. Not rest. Get here fast. Find things. I show." And he led the way through some thick grass to a pile of granite rocks. Behind the rocks were some very large bones.

"Monster bones!" said Wamba.

There was no mistaking what kind of bones Wamba had found. Breaking out into a cold sweat, Tony began to shiver.

"No, Wamba, those are snake bones!" he shuddered, cringing with fear. "Let's get out of here."

Before I could say anything to comfort Tony, Wilbur, who had taken the map from the chest, called us over to the log where he was standing.

"Come on up here," he said. "I want to show you something."

When we had climbed up onto the log, Wilbur pointed to a spot several yards beyond. Tony was standing right beside me, still trembling.

"Looks like some kind of cave," said Vera.

"I think it's the spot marked with an X on the map," said Wilbur.

"Well, there's a Frog Island and a Frog Mountain, but I still don't believe there's a treasure," said Albert. "Come on, let's find out once and for all."

In another moment we would all have jumped down from the log and run toward the cave, but something moved in the shadows. Wriggling through the rocks, two large snakes slithered into view. Tony gasped as they turned and disappeared into the tall grass. A second later another snake emerged. This one was even larger. Watching it enter the cave was like watching a long train pass by. It was clear to me now what the *SNA* and the *P* on the map stood for. No doubt the other letters that had been washed off were *KE* and *IT*. Put them together and they spell—*SNAKE PIT!*

(14)

"Looks like Grand Central Snake Station," said Albert. "Let's get out of here."

"We see monsters," agreed Boorha. "We leave now."

"You know we all want to help you, Pearl, but none of us bargained for this," said Vera. "That cave has wall-to-wall snakes. To go near it would be sheer suicide."

"You mean snakeicide," whined Tony. "Can we please get out of here?"

I looked at Wilbur and he lowered his eyes. Then I looked over toward the cave while another large python slithered in. I couldn't believe we had come so far only to give up. Yet how could we possibly go forward?

"Please," I said to everyone, "all I ask for is a few minutes to think. There's got to be some way to get in and out of that cave."

"If there were, I would have thought of it already," said Albert. "Don't waste your time. It's impossible."

"Maybe we could rush in, grab the emerald, and get out of there so fast they wouldn't be able to catch us," I said.

"No, that wouldn't work," said Vera. "Snakes are too fast for that."

For the moment we were safe. The breeze was blowing our scent away from the mouth of the cave and the snakes seemed to cluster toward the other side of the mountain.

"Snakes?" Boorha questioned us. *"You know snakes?"*

"Yes," replied Vera, "and they are not friendly toward mice."

"Yikes!" cried Tony, clutching at me for security. "Look! Coming toward us, there, in the grass, a snake!"

Something was moving in the grass. As it drew closer I recognized the ribbed pattern of a python sliding closer and closer.

"Run for it!" cried Albert. "Every mouse for himself!"

Boorha just laughed. Jumping down from the log, he ran toward the "snake."

Tony nearly fainted. But Boorha knew what he was doing. As the snake approached he reached out and grabbed hold of it with his paws. It wasn't really a snake. It was Wamba! While we were all preoccupied with looking at the cave, he had done a little more investigating and found a large snake skin. After pulling it over his head, he had dragged it along the ground with the intention of fooling us.

"Wamba find real monster skin." Wamba grinned sheepishly at his frowning father. "Make good costume for monster dance, yes, Poppa?"

Boorha was not amused. "You chief's son. Want grow up, be brave chief? Stay close. Not wander."

Time was running out, and Boorha's mice were growing anxious. Everyone was waiting for me to give the signal to go back down the mountain. If only I could think of something . . . some way to get past all those snakes. My mind was a blank. Though it didn't itch, I reached up and scratched my head. Perhaps I was trying to scratch up an idea like a chicken scratching up seeds in the dirt.

"I've got it!" I cried. "We have a snake skeleton and a snake skin. All we have to do is cover the skeleton with the snake skin, climb inside, and we're a snake! Then we can slither into the cave and no one will bother us."

For what seemed like a terribly long stretch of time, there was no response from anyone. Only stunned silence. Then Albert spoke:

"Well, if we could be mashed potatoes, there's no reason we couldn't be a snake. It's dangerous, but I have to admit I like the idea!"

"It's worth a try," said Vera.

I turned to Boorha.

"We help," he said.

Only Tony objected. "Go into that cave? You must be kidding!"

"This not like Tony. Wamba know Tony brave

mouse," said Wamba to Tony with a big smile. But Tony only shuddered.

"You don't have to go into the cave," I said to Tony. "You can go back down the mountain if you want to."

"No, I'll wait up here on the log," said Tony. "I don't want to go anywhere alone, not around here."

"Okay, you can be our lookout," I said. "If you see anything odd, let us know."

Our first task was to drag the snake skin Wamba had found over to the skeleton. It was very light, but we had to be careful not to snag or tear it. The skeleton was in perfect condition. Not a bone was missing and all its grim-looking teeth were firmly in place. Looking at it head-on in the grass, I couldn't shake the feeling that it was grinning at me. Starting at the tail end, we carefully slid the snake skin over the skeleton. The skin came from a slightly larger snake and hung loosely.

"Mr. Snake has too many wrinkles," complained Vera.

The name Mr. Snake stuck. From then on that's how we referred to our contraption.

"Not problem," said Boorha, and quickly set to work with his crew padding each of the rib bones with woven blades of grass. Using a thorn for a needle, they sewed the bottom of the snake skin so it fit tightly around the bones.

The skin was freshly molted and therefore flexible, but it was slow, tedious work. When the sun set we worked by moonlight. Only once in the middle of the night did we take a break. Most of us were hungry by then, yet with so many snakes around we didn't want to go far to forage. Luckily there were plenty of tasty roots nearby.

While we ate the wind shifted slightly and Tony was worried. "What if they smell us?"

"Don't worry," said Vera. "None of them have come this way so far. And I don't think they hunt at night."

"But it takes only one of those big garden hoses to eat the lot of us," complained Tony.

"I know how you feel," sympathized Wilbur, blowing his nose on a tiny leaf. "For a while I was feeling afraid of everything. Then I made up a little trick for myself."

"A trick?" asked Tony. "What kind of trick?"

"An easy trick," said Wilbur. "Maybe it will help you too. . . . Jay's mom has a blackboard in the kitchen where she writes notes and recipes, and sometimes Jay draws pictures on it. Whenever I'm afraid of something, I imagine that blackboard in my mind, then I draw a picture of what I'm afraid of on it. After I'm finished I take Jay's mom's sponge and wipe it clean, then I draw another picture—sometimes it's a rainbow, or a smiling face, or a flower. It doesn't matter so long as it makes the fear go away."

Tony screwed up his face and stroked his whiskers as if to say "Yeah, but will it work for snakes?"

"Look! Eyes for Mr. Snake," said Wamba, holding up two yellow berries that he had found on a nearby bush.

When all our stitching work was done, we stuck the

yellow berries in his empty eye sockets and Mr. Snake was complete.

Next we had to climb inside and figure out how to make Mr. Snake move. Since I was the one who could recognize the green emerald, I was the last to crawl into Mr. Snake's mouth. It was certainly an odd sensation to step over those sharp fangs into Mr. Snake's jaws of death. Settling myself in his mouth, I lowered the top portion of his skull and found that I could see quite nicely out of his nostrils.

"You look scary," Tony called down from the log.

"We feel scary," cried Wamba from deep within Mr. Snake's belly.

Our first efforts to get Mr. Snake to slither were a dismal failure. The best we could do was to make him writhe as if someone had stuck him with a fork.

"Wait a minute . . . this isn't working," I called back to everyone, and we all climbed out and had a conference. To get Mr. Snake to move like a real snake we had to push ourselves from one side to another in a coordinated way. So we worked out some tail signals. If I, as Mr. Snake's brain, wanted to go forward, I would signal the mouse behind me, Wilbur, with my tail. As he moved he would signal Vera, and so on down the line until the last mouse in Mr. Snake's tail knew what was going on and what he was supposed to do. This method greatly improved Mr. Snake's ability to move. With a little practice we could make him turn left or right, go forward, and turn completely around. Now his slither was acceptable, but no matter how hard we practiced we could manage only two speeds—slow and very slow.

"I hope we don't have to make a quick getaway," said Vera.

"What about smell?" worried Wilbur. "Mr. Snake looks okay, but I'm sure he smells an awful lot like mice."

"Or a snake with mouse-a-tosis," said Albert.

"What's mouse-a-tosis?" Boorha wanted to know.

"Mouse breath," replied Albert.

It had taken us quite a while to construct Mr. Snake and figure out how to make him move. In a little while the sun would rise and the snakes, cold-blooded creatures that they were, would become more active. It was time to go.

As Albert climbed into Mr. Snake he mumbled out loud, "I can't believe I'm doing this, risking my life for a kid I don't even know."

"You'd like him if you knew him," I said. "Maybe after this is all over you and Vera can come back to Jay's house. Who knows? He might like having four pet mice."

From the disgusted look Albert gave me, I could tell it was the wrong thing to say and the worst time to say it.

Slowly, with a solemn air, mouse after mouse climbed into Mr. Snake's mouth.

"Wait a minute. I don't want to stay here alone," cried Tony.

"Good, Tony!" cried Wamba. "I brave, you brave. We brave brothers."

It took some last-minute rearranging, but soon Tony was settled in with the rest of us. At last we were all ready. Climbing into Mr. Snake's mouth, I flicked my tail and gave the signal to move forward.

(15)

As we slithered toward the cave the reddish glow of the rising sun colored the rocks and plants in our path as surely as if an artist's brush had dabbed them all with bright red paint. It was not far to the cave, but since my vision was limited by what I could see through Mr. Snake's nostrils, I was not always sure we were headed in the right direction. Twice we almost bumped head-on into some rocks. This hadn't happened when we practiced.

"Pearl, you've got to concentrate," I said to myself. "Stop thinking about what's ahead and watch where you're going."

It seemed to take us forever to get to the cave. I was beginning to worry that somehow we had gotten turned around. Then I caught a glimpse of the mouth of the cave.

"Are we there yet?" Wilbur whispered from behind.

"Almost," I replied.

Though we hadn't planned it that way, the angle of the sun was perfect. As we entered it shone directly into the cave—a red beacon to guide our way.

We hadn't gone very far when we encountered a large python exiting from the cave. He must have been three times the size of Mr. Snake. The expression on his face was a sour one. As his massive head pulled alongside ours he flicked his tongue in our direction and hissed.

"You sssmell like mice."

My response was critical. If I said the wrong thing, we'd never get beyond this point.

"Yesss," I replied, lowering my voice as much as possible, "the hunting was good yesssterday."

Again the large snake flicked his tongue in my direction. "I don't believe I've ever sssseen you around here before."

This snake was definitely suspicious, and I got the feeling he was trying to test me. I dared not risk another reply. Pretending not to hear him at all, I flicked my tail three times, giving the signal to increase speed.

It was very damp but surprisingly warm in the cave. Water glistened on its walls and dripped to the clay floor, turning it muddy in places.

Several yards into the cave I noticed an enormous boa constrictor coming toward us. His width was twice that of a man's leg and he seemed to go on forever! His sheer bulk was so alarming, I got flustered and made a terrible mistake. Flicking my tail two times to the right instead of one time to the left, rather than steering around this monument of a reptile, we collided.

"Watch it, sssmall fry!" he hissed.

"Ssssorry," I replied, unable to hide the fear in my voice.

No doubt accustomed to the terror he inspired in others, the huge snake did not reply. He merely narrowed his eyes and flicked his tongue. Hastily I gave the signal to go forward and we slid past his scaly coils.

"What's going on?" whispered Wilbur from behind.

"Tell ya later," I whispered back.

"Tell me what later," I heard a voice hiss from above.

Lifting Mr. Snake's head slightly, I caught a glimpse of a bright orange snake perched upon an outcropping of rock above us. Sliding forward, she dropped down to our level.

"Well, ssspeak!" she flicked her tongue, which was also bright orange. "Or do you talk only to yourssssself?"

She was slightly larger or perhaps even the same size as Mr. Snake, but her manner was so smug and saucy, I surmised that she was extremely poisonous.

Imitating her haughty tone of voice, I replied, "I didn't sssay anything, misss, pleasssse sssslide out of my way," and continued on into the cave.

"Sssstop!" she cried, but I didn't even slow down. Hurriedly we passed some other snakes without mishap. But we hadn't gone very far when the orange snake slithered up beside us.

"You misssunderssstand," she said. "There's sssomething about you that I find sssimply irresssissstible."

I didn't know what to say or how to respond. A few yards up ahead, where the cave widened into a large chamber, I caught a glimpse of a bright yellow light. At first I was puzzled. What could it be? Then I realized what I was looking at. It was an enormous pile of gold coins, rings, bracelets, and other objects all made of gold. And on top of this gleaming yellow heap of wealth was the treasure chest! It looked just like the one I'd seen in the crystal ball!

"I am sssorry," I said to the orange snake, "but I am sssomewhat ssshy. Give me ssssome time to collect myssssself and I will meet you ssshortly, outssside. Then we will talk sssome more."

"Whatever you sssay," hissed the orange snake as she turned to leave. "I will count the ssseconds until we meet again. I find your company sssso pleasurable. Pleassse make it ssssoon, my ssssweet."

When she was gone Wilbur whispered impatiently, "What's going on?"

"I just made a date with an orange snake," I replied.

"That's all we need . . . a date with an orange snake," said Wilbur. "Now we have something to look forward to. What about the treasure?"

"It's only a few yards up ahead, but there's a carpet of snakes all around it." I spoke as quietly as I could.

Wilbur didn't reply, but I felt a bead of sweat from his brow drip onto my tail. Taking a deep breath, I gave the signal to move forward.

"A carpet of snakes" was no exaggeration, for that's exactly what we encountered as we approached the pile of gold. Somehow the treasure itself had attracted all the snakes to this chamber. Though they had no use for it, they seemed to enjoy merely being in its presence. No doubt that explained why they preferred to stay near the top of Frog Mountain and never bothered Boorha and his tribe in the valley.

Sliding over the intertwined bodies of hundreds of snakes, we moved slowly and awkwardly toward the pile of gold.

"Hey, missster!" hissed a cobra, spreading its hood. "Watch your ssssstep!"

"Sssorry, excussse me. No offenssssse," I was forced to say again and again, but we moved steadily forward until at last we reached the edge of the pile of gold.

The pile was steep and difficult for Mr. Snake to ascend. More than once we climbed several feet only to slide down again, tumbling in the yellowness. Though Mr. Snake was taking quite a lot of punishment, he was holding up fine. As we neared our goal I felt my heart quicken with the excitement of being so close to the treasure and the green emerald. Finally we rounded the top of the pile.

At last! We had arrived at the treasure chest. Protruding from the pile of gold, it reminded me of a giant tree stump cut close to the ground. But what a tree stump it was, like something from a fairy tale! Precious gems as big as rocks flowed over its sides and onto the pile of gold like so much popcorn. Even though it was very dark in the cave, each and every gem glistened like a raindrop in bright sunlight!

Guiding Mr. Snake up onto one of these piles, I signaled to give an extra push, and we eased up into the chest, spilling some of the treasure onto the pile of gold and down to the snakes below.

But where was the green emerald? I saw many emeralds through Mr. Snake's nostrils, but not the one I was looking for—the special one I had seen in the crystal ball. How could that be? Had someone been here already and taken it?

"It's not here. It's gone," I whispered to Wilbur.

"But it's got to be there. Dig for it," he answered.

That meant crawling out into the open. Trembling, I raised Mr. Snake's jaw and peeked out between his fangs.

"Come on!" Wilbur poked me from behind.

"Okay, okay," I squeaked, and dived headfirst out of Mr. Snake and into the treasure.

My first impulse was to bury myself. Throwing rubies, diamonds, and all kinds of precious stones this way and that, I soon had myself covered up to my neck in treasure. It was like taking a billion-dollar bubble bath. But I couldn't very well look for the emerald and hide at the same time. Below me I could see all the snakes gathered around the pile of gold and I couldn't help but shudder at the thought of what would happen if one of them should spot me.

Easing out of my hiding place, I dug into the treasure, searching desperately for the green emerald. But the chest was so enormous, it seemed hopeless.

"I can't find it!" I called to Wilbur.

"It's got to be there," he answered, and crawled out of Mr. Snake's mouth to help me look.

With two mice walking around out in the open, I was really scared. I was trembling so much, I couldn't get my paws to work right. In desperation I tried Wilbur's trick with the blackboard. In my mind's eye I quickly drew a snake with me in its mouth. Then I erased it and drew a picture of me in Jay's hands. That calmed me down considerably. Though I wasn't shaking anymore, I was still scared.

Minutes passed and we seemed no nearer our goal than when we began. How could we possibly find one emerald in such a huge chest—if indeed it was here at all?

"Is this it?" Wilbur asked again and again. "How about this one?"

Every time he asked I had to tell him no. I was beginning to wonder what it was I had really seen in the crystal ball. While Wilbur kept digging I closed my eyes and tried to calm down some more.

The emerald *was* here. I could feel it pulling at me with invisible strings. Keeping my eyes closed, I let the emerald guide me to itself. As I got closer I could sense its presence more and more. Finally I reached down, cast a few diamonds aside, and saw it—the green emerald!

It looked even more beautiful than when I had seen

it in the crystal ball. For a moment, in spite of the danger, I stood in awe just staring at it. So green, so powerful, so peaceful, in an instant all the fear inside of me melted away to nothing.

"Wilbur, I found it!" I cried, and scooped it up in my arms. Clutching it to my chest, I felt like I was holding something alive, like a flower or a newborn baby mouse. Closing my eyes, I felt it pulsing like a heartbeat. The longer I kept my eyes closed, the stronger the pulse became. It was so soothing, like a sweet lullaby, I had to force myself to open my eyes.

When I did I saw something I hadn't noticed before. Beyond the main chamber, farther on into the cave, I saw a patch of clear blue sky. That meant there was another way out of the cave. It was certainly a shorter route and hopefully it would be safer too.

Meanwhile, Wilbur was standing next to me staring at the emerald.

"So that's it," he said. "Doesn't look special to me."

"It doesn't?" I was utterly amazed.

"Well, it is pretty," said Wilbur. "If you're sure it's the right one, I say let's get out of here."

When we got back into Mr. Snake's mouth, I passed the emerald back to Wilbur and it was time to leave. Before I gave the signal to move ahead I reached out and scooped up as much treasure as I could. My intention was to take it back down the mountain as a gift for Lowpa and the entire village.

"After all," I thought to myself as I gathered up another load of treasure, "without the help of Boorha

and his mice, I doubt we could have gotten Mr. Snake to move at all, let alone slither." Unfortunately, feeling both grateful and generous, I got carried away and stuffed Mr. Snake with too much treasure.

If his movements seemed awkward before, he was downright clumsy now. Instead of sliding out of the chest, we fell out of it, rolling down the pile of gold and bumping into the carpet of snakes.

"Hey! Watch your step! Sssscram!" said one irate snake.

"Sssorry," I kept apologizing as I clinked and clanked along.

"What happened to you?" said a medium-sized anaconda. "You look like you jusssst ate a rockpile."

As we traveled across the carpet of snakes the sound of diamonds, rubies, and sapphires knocking against one another and Mr. Snake's bulging sides drew a great deal of attention.

"I haven't ssssseen you around here before," hissed a suspicious boa constrictor. "And you ssssmell more like a nesssst of mice than any ssssnake I've ever met."

"Pleassse leave me alone, I'm feeling sssick," I said, but that only aroused more curiosity.

"Your ssskin doesssn't look healthy, sssir," said one well-meaning snake. "It looksssss like it'ssss already been ssshed."

When we left the carpet of snakes around the pile of gold, instead of heading out of the cave the way we came in, I guided Mr. Snake toward the other entrance I had seen from atop the treasure chest. Slowly Mr.

Snake climbed the gentle incline that led toward the ever-widening patch of blue sky.

After the fearful darkness of the cave, the deep azure sky was indeed a welcome sight. Sliding up the moist earth like a worm coming up to the surface, we left the cave behind and continued on.

"We're out!" I called back to Wilbur. "We did it!"

"Did what?" called a voice from behind.

I flicked my tail and gave the signal to turn. Behind us were several large snakes, a giant python, three or four boa constrictors, and numerous anacondas. Suspicious of Mr. Snake's odd appearance, they had followed us out of the cave!

"You're very sssstrange," hissed the giant python. "Why is it that we never sssee your tongue?"

"Yesss, let'sssssee your tongue," demanded one of the larger boa constrictors. "If you have one, that isss."

We hadn't thought to provide Mr. Snake with a tongue. A simple blade of grass would have done the trick.

"Well," hissed the python, edging menacingly toward me, "let's sssee it."

I was sure they were onto our trick, so I had to do something and I had to do it quick.

"Of courssssse I have a tongue," I said, and in sheer desperation I thrust my paw out of Mr. Snake's mouth and instantly jerked it back.

"That wassss no tongue," said one of the anacondas.

"It looked very sssstrange to me," hissed the python.

"Open your mouth. I want to sssee what'sss really in-ssside."

"Sssstrange? How absssurd! There'sss nothing sssstrange about me, I asssure you," I replied indignantly, and gave the signal to move forward. My haughty stance might have worked, but just then we bumped headfirst into a big rock, which shook Mr. Snake's eyes loose and popped them right out of their sockets onto the ground!

"Sssso, you are an imposssster! Jussst as we ssssussspected!" hissed the python, and all the other snakes moved to surround us, blocking any avenue of escape. Helplessly turning Mr. Snake's head from side to side, I watched while the circle of serpents around us grew smaller and smaller.

Slowly pulling back his head, the python drew itself into a coil, ready to strike. At any moment I expected to feel the impact of his fangs. My body tensed. But instead of attacking, the python arched its head skyward, recoiled in fear, and slithered away into the cave. Miraculously, without a word being spoken, all the other snakes followed him.

I didn't know what was going on, but I breathed a sigh of relief. As I did I felt a gush of air and something grabbed Mr. Snake from behind and lifted us into the air!

(16)

"WHAT HAPPENED?" CRIED WILBUR.

"We're in the air. It must be a bird," I called back. "We'd better pretend Mr. Snake is dead. Go limp, and tell the others to do the same."

Turning first one way then another as it adjusted itself to the wind, the bird glided down Frog Mountain. For the longest time all I could see out of Mr. Snake's nostrils was bright blue sky. It was a frightful situation and I was utterly terrified. But another part of me was enjoying the ride. Trembling with fear, I thought to myself, "So this is flying!"

Then I saw the leaves of many branches rush past.

"Hungry! Hungry! Hungry!" cried the bird's three fledglings as it dropped us into its nest.

The fledglings had large heads and fluffy feathers of brilliant indigo. They weren't hawks or owls or parrots but some kind of rare jungle bird. Leaving Mr. Snake as food for its fledglings to feast on, the beautiful parent bird launched itself gracefully into the air to join its mate, circling high above. Soaring into the sunlight, the two purple-feathered birds rose higher and higher like intertwining streams of smoke spiraling into the sky.

Meanwhile, the chicks wasted no time. With their sharp beaks they ripped open Mr. Snake as if he were a Christmas present wrapped in tissue paper.

"Mine! Mine! Mine!" they shrieked, until we all tumbled out. Then they drew back in stunned silence. Bewildered, they tilted their heads from side to side and stared at one another blankly.

"Quick," cried Boorha, and he led his mice over the rim of the nest and out onto the limb of the tree where the nest was secured.

"Tree bark rough, easy to climb down," I heard Wamba say as Tony, Albert, and Vera followed the others.

Only Wilbur and I remained in the nest, frantically searching through the remains of Mr. Snake for the green emerald.

"It's got to be here," said Wilbur, tossing a large sapphire to the ground.

"There it is!" I saw the emerald glimmering under a shredded flap of snake skin. I ran over to it, hastily scooped it up in my paws, and heaved it out of the nest.

Meanwhile, the fledglings had regained their composure. Perhaps we were not the sumptuous meal they had expected, but we were something good to eat. As Wilbur and I were about to jump out of the nest one of the fledglings thrust his beak toward us and knocked us down.

"Are you okay?" cried Wilbur.

"Yeah, I'm all right," I answered, struggling to regain my breath, for the wind had been knocked out of me.

"I think we're their first live food," said Wilbur, helping me to my feet.

"Personally, I'd rather not think of it that way," I gasped.

All three birds were staring at us, waiting for us to make a move. Slowly we turned and started to climb up the side of the nest again.

This time one of the other birds struck out at Wilbur, torpedoing him in the shoulder. Falling backward, he knocked me down and we were right back where we started.

"They want to kill us but they don't know how. So they're waiting for one of their parents to come back and do it for them," said Wilbur.

"I think you're right. I'll distract them while you make a run for it."

"No! I won't leave you!" protested Wilbur. "We'll get out of this together or not at all."

For a few minutes or so we stood facing the fledglings. It was a terrible standoff. They didn't know how to kill us and we didn't know how to get away. Then Wilbur got an idea.

"Remember the parakeets in Adams's Pet Store?" he said, picking up a sparkling white diamond from the

floor of the nest. "Remember how they loved anything shiny?"

"Yes, I remember," I said, recalling the tiny silver bells that Mr. Adams sold for them to peck at.

Turning the diamond in his paws, Albert flashed a bright ray of sunlight in one of the fledglings' eyes. The young bird responded at once. Craning his head forward on his rubbery neck, he stared at the diamond with rapt attention.

"What if I were to throw this diamond in their direction?" said Wilbur. "Do you think it would distract them long enough for us to get out of here?"

"It's worth a try," I answered.

"Okay." Wilbur sighed heavily. "As soon as I throw it we'll make a run for it. Ready? One, two, three!" And he heaved the diamond. It was an excellent throw. As the glittering gem spun toward the fledglings' feet it cast sparks of white light into their eyes. The combination of movement and light proved irresistible. All at once the fledglings fell upon the diamond, pecking ferociously.

"Mine! Mine! Mine!" they screeched.

"Okay! Now!" cried Wilbur. Like inmates scaling the walls of a prison, we scrambled out of the nest and jumped down onto the crotch of the tree. When we reached the ground, the others were waiting for us.

"We were worried," said Vera. "I was about to go up and see what happened."

"The fledglings got a little feisty," said Wilbur, rubbing his shoulder, "but we're okay now."

"Purple bird give big favor," said Boorha with a smile. "Take us down mountain. Village not far. Come. I show way."

Though most of the treasure we had collected in the cave remained in the nest, we had no trouble finding the emerald and the sapphire Wilbur and I had thrown to the ground.

When we got back to the camp, I put the emerald in a safe place and presented the sapphire to Lowpa.

"It's for you and the whole village," I said.

"Sapphire beautiful," said Lowpa as she accepted our gift. "Hard like stone but soft like flower."

That evening there was another celebration, and Boorha himself performed with the rest of the tribe. Wearing an elaborate costume made of woven grass, Boorha and a dozen or so mice acted out the drama we'd lived earlier that day. Performed to the steady rhythm of loud drumming, Boorha's dance depicted our entire adventure in the cave up to and including our escape from the fledglings.

After the dance Boorha announced, "Now wisdom of present joins wisdom of past, let us seek wisdom of future."

Then Lowpa presented me with a present wrapped in a flower petal and tied with a strand of grass. Inside was a beautiful white pearl the size of a pea.

"I find on beach one day," she said. "Until you give sapphire, it most beautiful thing Lowpa have."

"Please don't ask me to take this," I said. "It's too beautiful."

"I want to give this white stone when you first come to village . . . when you return Wamba," she said. "I could not give then. That trouble me. Now I give freely."

I had never held a real pearl in my paws before, or ever dreamed of owning one. It was so smooth and pure, so milky white, like something from out of the sky, yet it felt like a part of me . . . like my own tail or nose. I accepted Lowpa's gift and, rubbing our whiskers together, thanked her from the bottom of my heart.

Though I wouldn't have believed it possible, this celebration was even more festive than the one we had witnessed before. Best of all, we were allowed to participate. Though Wilbur and I were still somewhat sore from the blows we had received earlier, Tony and the others danced far into the night, beating on the drums until the sun rose the next morning.

After resting for a day and a night in the village, I informed Boorha and Lowpa that we had to leave.

"Wherever you go, remember this also your home," said Boorha.

Later that afternoon, while we loaded up the dinghy, Lowpa came to me.

"My Wamba and little Tony good friends now," she began. "Like roots of tree and earth, they give good things to one another."

"Yes," I replied, "it will be sad to part them."

Wamba, who was not far away, overheard what Lowpa and I had said.

"Wamba not leave Tony. Wamba go in boat and see big world," he declared.

Lowpa looked at me as if to ask "Is that possible?"

"I see no reason why he couldn't come with us," I said, "but it's up to you and Boorha to make the decision."

"I like you see more big world," said Lowpa to Wamba, "but you promise come back to village. You chief's son. Someday you chief."

"Wamba come back, yes!" Wamba replied.

Lowpa had a long talk with Boorha. At first he was very much opposed to the idea.

"My father and his father before him never leave island," he argued with Lowpa. "They all good chiefs. Sun and sky, earth and spirits of jungle give us everything. What good see big world? How we know Wamba come back?"

"But Wamba promise, Wamba come back and be good chief," pleaded Wamba.

In the end Boorha agreed and gave Wamba his blessing, saying, "I not know if this wise. Only one way find out. Let Wamba go."

Tony and Wamba were jubilant. Standing upright and holding each other's front paws, they jumped up and down in a circle.

At his request we ferried Boorha out to the *Golden Hind* to meet Old Bill.

"This floating hut like jungle flower," he said as he climbed onto the deck of the *Golden Hind.* "Pretty, but I like flower have roots."

Old Bill was delighted to have Wamba as a new crew member.

"We can always use another set of paws," he told Wamba. "But you must remember, as long as you are on this ship, I am chief."

"Wamba make big promise, always follow orders from ship chief."

At this Boorha smiled. "Our ancestors have saying. 'One ant cannot build anthill. All must work together.' "

Old Bill said all the right things to reassure Boorha that Wamba would be well looked after. By the time Boorha returned to the shore he was even joking about becoming a sailor someday.

As we pulled up the anchor the entire village came to see us off. Waving from the beach, they all held paws and sang us a good-bye song. Though I don't remember the exact words, it went something like:

> In the morning the sun sends the stars away.
> They are leaving.
> But they do not say good-bye.
> When the seed grows into a tree,
> It is leaving.
> But it does not say good-bye.
> When the flowers close their petals at night,
> They are leaving.
> But they do not say good-bye.
> When will we see your face?

When will we hear your voice?
When will our whiskers touch again?
You are leaving.
But we will not say good-bye.

(17)

As soon as we set sail my first concern was to find a safe place to keep the emerald. I know it sounds silly, but to me it was like a guest and I wanted to make it feel comfortable and safe. First I checked down in the hold, but that was too dark and gloomy. Then I thought of the crystal ball. There was plenty of room in the captain's cedar chest. "Perhaps the emerald and the crystal ball would enjoy each other's company," I thought to myself. So I took the emerald to the captain's cabin.

Going over to the cedar chest, I lifted the lid.

"Hello, crystal ball, I brought a friend for you," I said, and resting the emerald on the bed, I took the crystal ball from its black velvet bag. Then I placed the crystal ball next to the emerald and took some things out of the chest to make room.

When I was finished I turned around and was amazed to find the crystal ball glowing with a faint blue light. In the light was an image. I drew closer and the image became more distinct. I saw a room and a bed. I reached out and pulled the crystal ball closer. It was a hospital room. And there was a person in the bed. It was Jay! All around the bed were gray machines with blinking red lights and wires and tubes connected to Jay's wrists and stomach and head.

"Jay's still sick," I thought to myself. "Oh, poor Jay!" While I watched the door to the hospital room opened and Jay's mother came in. In her hands she held a brightly wrapped package. She looked so tired. Her eyes seemed dark, and her lips were stretched tightly across her face.

"Happy birthday, Jay," said his mom, and she put the package down on the bed. But Jay didn't open the package. He didn't even look at it. He just lay there and stared straight ahead.

"Oh please, Jay, get better," I said, and found myself reaching out for the emerald.

Holding it close, I closed my eyes and took a deep breath. The emerald made me feel so calm, time itself seemed to stop. I could smell the sea breeze gently streaming in through the porthole and hear the busy sounds of everyone on deck, but I felt so far away, like a snail drawn into its shell.

I felt the emerald pressing against my chest and saw its green light shining inside of me. Love. It poured through me from someplace beyond, like a gush of water bubbling out of a deep well.

"Let this love heal Jay," I prayed out loud, and somehow I knew my prayer was being answered.

When I opened my eyes and looked into the crystal ball, I saw Jay again. He had picked up the package and was opening it.

Not long after we left Frog Island Albert finished his *Mouseifesto.*

"It's done!" he cried one day, running around the deck like a madmouse. "It's done, it's done, it's done!"

"Good!" exclaimed Vera. "Now we can travel with Old Bill, Tony, and Wamba—that is if you haven't changed your mind."

"Of course not!" replied Albert, then he turned to Wilbur. "Are you coming with us?"

"Ah . . . er, I'm not sure," said Wilbur.

"We can always use another set of paws to sail the *Golden Hind,*" said Old Bill.

"Just think of the adventure of it all," said Vera.

"What do you say, Pearl?" Wilbur turned to me. "Shall we?"

"That little boy of yours doesn't even know your real names, or if you're a boy or a girl mouse," said Albert.

"I can't speak for Wilbur," I said, "but my answer is thanks but no thanks. I've got to go back."

"But, Pearl . . ." Wilbur reached out to touch my paw. I turned away.

"Well, Supernose?" said Albert. "What's your answer? You going to be a pet mouse all your life or come away with us?"

"I don't know," replied Wilbur. "I have to think about it."

That evening Albert asked me if I knew Jay's mailing address.

"Sure," I told him. "I watched him write it on the upper left-paw corner whenever he wrote a letter to his pen pal."

"Good," said Albert. "Then my plan will work."

Albert's plan was simple. Instead of sailing north, we would head the *Golden Hind* west until we hit the coast. Then we'd sail up the coast until we found a little town.

"We're bound to find a post office in almost any town," said Albert. "Then all we have to do is pop you into a box and send you home."

I realized it was a risky way to travel, but so was sailing. At least this way would be fast. A few days later we steered the ship into a bay off the mainland and dropped anchor amid some tall reeds. When we had loaded up the dinghy with the emerald, the crystal ball, and the pearl, Old Bill said:

"Well, lass, I reckon we'll be saying good-bye now."

"Thanks for helping," I said, and gave him a big hug.

"You're welcome, lass," he replied, and squeezed me so hard, I thought my bones would break. "For a mouse you're a lot like a cat"—he smiled—"always landing on your feet. May your sails always be full and your rudder never run aground."

As we rowed toward the beach and the little town, I

couldn't take my eyes off the *Golden Hind*. She looked so beautiful with her white sails against the moonlit sky. I expected to be sad about leaving Old Bill. What I didn't expect was to be so sad about leaving the *Golden Hind*. For the first time I think I got an inkling of how Old Bill felt about *Gertrude*.

After coming ashore and hiding the dinghy, we made our way into town. It was a small town, with one gas station, two churches, and a few stores. But no post office. At least we couldn't find it. Then we realized it was in the grocery store. That same store also had a soda fountain and sold sporting goods.

"Some grocery store," commented Tony as he slid under the door, "they've got everything in here."

"What *grocery store* mean?" asked Wamba, and Tony did his best to explain.

"A grocery store is where people buy things . . ." he began.

"What *buy* mean? What *people* be?" asked Wamba.

Our first task was to find a suitable box to send me home in. There were several to choose from in the wastepaper basket.

"This one's too big for one mouse," I said to Wilbur, pointing to one of the boxes, "but it would be just right for two."

Without saying anything, Wilbur jumped into the wastepaper basket and started tugging on the box.

"You're coming with me?" I asked.

"Yes, I've made my decision," answered Wilbur.

"You mean you don't mind being a *pet mouse* all your life?"

Wilbur stopped what he was doing and looked me straight in the eye. "Well, I've thought about it. The words *pet mouse* are just words if you're doing what you want to do."

We had quite a struggle getting that box out of the wastepaper basket and onto the floor, but the rest was easy. We found everything we needed—labels, postage, string, brown wrapping paper, and ink on a shelf in the post office part of the store.

While Wilbur helped Albert write out the address label, Vera helped me pack the crystal ball, the emerald, and my pearl in tissue paper. These were things I just couldn't leave behind. On one of the shelves in the grocery section we found some crackers for the trip. Wamba and Tony chewed open the package and carried the crackers one by one to my box.

"Crackers, good food!" exclaimed Wamba. "Where crackers grow?"

Soon everything was ready and there was nothing left to do but climb in the box and say good-bye.

"Take good care of Wamba," I said, hugging Tony. "And don't give Old Bill a hard time."

Tony cast his eyes down and was silent. I could tell he was feeling sad and holding back the tears. But I couldn't resist hugging him again, even if it did make him cry.

Then Wilbur and I rubbed whiskers and hugged Albert. "Will you write us letters?" I asked. "You have Jay's address."

"Sure," he replied, "if you answer them."

"I can't promise," I said, "but I'll try."

"You know sometimes I wish we were sisters," said Vera as she gave me a good-bye hug.

"But, Vera, I feel like we're sisters already," I replied.

"Wamba sad," said Wamba. "I miss Pearl and Wilbur and they not even gone yet."

"And we'll miss you," I said. "We'll miss you all."

"Well, come on," cried Wilbur. "The sun'll be up soon. We'd better get in the box now!"

As soon as I climbed in Albert handed me a piece of paper. "It's the treasure map. I thought you might like to have it. I wrote a note on the back of it for Jay."

I was about to read the note when Vera closed the flaps to our box, saying, "Good luck, and smooth sailing."

Outside we could hear everyone tying the box with string and sticking on the address label and stamps. When they were done we shouted, "Good-bye!" and they all shouted back, "Good-bye!" Then everything was quiet.

"What's this package doing here?" said the postmaster a few hours later when he found our box lying on the floor in front of his window.

"I hope he doesn't shake us to see what's inside," worried Wilbur.

He did shake us, but only a little. Then he canceled

our stamps, the very ones we had taken from his shelf, and set us down to wait for the afternoon mail truck.

"Remember how you felt when you realized we were on the way to France?" asked Wilbur.

"Oh! Don't remind me."

"But it did work out all for the best, didn't it? If we hadn't gotten trapped in that crate, we never would have found the emerald."

"But we don't really know if the emerald did any good or not," I replied gloomily. Listening to my own voice, I realized how depressed I was feeling.

"Think we'll ever see Albert, Vera, Tony, Old Bill, and Wamba again?" I wondered out loud.

"Hard to say," said Wilbur, swallowing a lump in his throat. I could tell he was feeling just as sad as I was.

After a while we lost track of whether it was night or day. They kept moving us from one place to another. One time I think we went on a conveyor belt but I wasn't sure. I know they put us on an airplane though. We could tell from the sounds of other planes taking off. It didn't really feel like we were flying.

"Someday I'd like to go on a real airplane ride, one where we could look out the windows and see the ground below," I said to Wilbur.

"Yeah, that would be nice," sighed Wilbur. "You know I've been thinking. It's been a long time since the accident. If Jay's better, he might have gotten some new mice by now."

At first I rejected Wilbur's suggestion, but the more

I thought about it, the more I had to admit it *was* possible.

"What if we don't like these new mice?" fretted Wilbur. "What if Jay likes them more than us? And what if they tease me about 'Sally'?"

I don't know how long the trip took, several days, perhaps even a week. But we were getting down to our last cracker when we finally arrived at Jay's house. For all we knew we were in some post office somewhere. We were so used to getting picked up and jostled about, we had learned to sleep through it all. And that's what we were doing when Jay opened our box—sleeping.

I can still remember that moment so vividly. All of a sudden our box was flooded with sunshine. Squinting sleepily, we looked up and there was Jay's face beaming down at us with a smile as bright as the sun itself.

"George! Sally! You're back!"

Oh, Mouse! He was so happy, and so were we!

Reaching down into the box, he picked us up in his hands.

"I missed you both so much. I was very sick, you know. In a coma for weeks and weeks. But then on my birthday I pulled out of it. And since then I've been getting stronger and stronger."

"As if we didn't know," said Wilbur to me with a sly wink.

We were in Jay's bedroom. I can't describe how wonderful it felt to see it again. Everything was so familiar. At last we were home! But there was something new too. Standing up, Jay carried us over to the windowsill and showed us his new pets.

"When I got better, Mom wanted to buy me two new mice. But I wouldn't let her. She said you were probably dead. But I knew better. I let her get me some goldfish though. Kinda cute, don't you think? I haven't given them names yet. Mom's at a meeting. Boy is she going to be surprised when she sees you two!"

Then Jay took us to our cage. It was still on the little table next to his bed. I wanted to go in our cage and curl up in the cup we always slept in. But more than that, I wanted to stay close to Jay.

Jay was so excited. He kept skipping and hopping around the room, showing us different things, like the twisted handlebars of his old bicycle.

"The rest of the bike was a wreck," he said, "but I kept this as a souvenir of the accident."

Finally Jay set us down on his desk and looked in the box we came in. He didn't notice the map, but he did read the note:

Dear Jay,
You must be a really good kid to be loved so much by your pet mice. The world needs more people like you. Don't grow up to be a rat!
                              Signed,
                              A Friend
P.S. You got their names wrong. It's not Sally and George, but Wilbur and Pearl.

Setting down the note, Jay picked me up.

"Then you must be Wilbur," he said. "I'm sorry I got your name wrong."

"Darn it!" squeaked Wilbur. "Now he's going to call me Pearl for the rest of my life! I can't stand it!" And he ran over to the cardboard box, which was tipped on its side.

"Now where is it?" he cried, rummaging through the box. "Ah, here it is!" He emerged from the box with the pearl Lowpa had given me. Running over to Jay's hand, he placed the pearl in my paws. Then he squeaked loudly again and again.

"She's not Wilbur, she's Pearl. I'm Wilbur."

Jay listened to Wilbur squeak for some time.

"I think you're trying to tell me something."

"He sure is," I squeaked.

Then Wilbur started running up and down in a zig-zag pattern that looked a lot like the letter W.

"W for Wilbur," he squeaked again and again. "Get it? Wilbur! I'm Wilbur!"

"MMMM," said Jay, reminding me of Captain Mc-Call. "I've got it! You must be Pearl! That's why Wilbur gave you the pearl!" Then he scooped up Wilbur and, holding us both up close to his face, gently rubbed his cheek against our fur.

"I can't believe it! Jay finally knows our real names," I cried.

"Well it's about time," sighed Wilbur.

"I'll never figure out how you got here," said Jay, and he reached into the box and took out the crystal ball.

Closing one eye, he held it up to the other and looked through it.

"Not a bad shooter," he said, and dropped it into the tin can on his bureau, where he kept his marbles. Then he found the emerald. "Kinda neat, but too big to be real," he said, and put it in the old shoe box under his bed, where he kept his collection of seashells and broken glass.